# A BERMUDA TRIANGLE
## *Love Story*

### BY
# PAUL FERRANTE

*A Bermuda Triangle Love Story*, Copyright 2019 Paul Ferrante
Published by The Ionian Press
Cover by Carol Young/The Creative Barn
Layout by www.formatting4U.com

For more information on the author and his works, please see www.PaulFerranteAuthor.com.

Digital ISBN: 978-1-7324857-4-7
Print ISBN: 978-1-7324857-5-4

This book is also available in print at online retailers.

# Dedication

To Matty
Brothers in arms…
Partners in crime…
Friends forever.

# Acknowledgments

It takes a village…
Special thanks to Carrie Ferrante for her editorial
expertise and pithy remarks, Carol Young at the
Creative Barn
for the cover art, author Denise Devine Meinstad
for her continued guidance, and Judi
Fennell@formatting4U.com
for answering my plethora of questions.
And finally, to the wonderful people of Bermuda:
I hope to visit you again.

# Chapter One

Finally.

After forty-two years of having to travel during peak times, Bobby Romero was flying in September, when all the kids—and their poor teachers, a brotherhood to which he formerly belonged—were back at school. He'd hated having to deal with all the price gouging the airlines imposed upon those who were locked into school break weeks, and the cattle car-like atmosphere the overbooked flights created. And then there was the feeling at the end of your week or ten days when you started worrying about the next week's lesson plans and those few pain in the butt students you had every year that you'd been given a blessed reprieve from. Before you knew it you'd be back to work, back on the treadmill.

But no more. *Hello, retirement.*

Bobby had planned well. His exit strategy had begun a few years before, with the help of a good retirement advisor and, of course, Valentina, who was a whiz at all things financial. In fact, Bobby hadn't had to balance a checkbook or pay a bill since they'd been married over thirty years ago. Which made sense, since she had started her business career in banking. In fact, they'd met in his hometown bank on a school holiday when he'd gone in to cash his meager private school check for teaching tenth grade English and coaching junior varsity high school football in the Bronx.

Of course, he'd noticed her before. Bobby always had an eye out for attractive girls, and Valentina Dominguez certainly rated a second look. She stood at barely five feet, with long black hair and big brown eyes that somehow exuded kindness and serenity. And from what he could see from above the counter, she was also pretty well-built, always a Romero prerequisite. When he stopped in to do his banking, he always tried to maneuver into her line to check her out. And she was always pleasant to him, like she was to everybody.

So, on that fateful day in November, he'd mustered up the courage to ask her for a date, breaking the string of aimless one-nighters he'd engaged in since *The Disaster*. Not knowing how else to do it, and always having been more adept with a pen than with his mouth, he'd scribbled a note on the back of a deposit slip asking if he could have her phone number. When he'd pushed it across the counter and said, "I think you should read this," her beautiful Spanish eyes had widened and she'd blushed. The people behind him on line must've thought he was trying to rob the bank or something (in fact, she later told him she had her foot on the alarm button under the counter that was wired to the local police station, fearing the same thing). But, in a prodigious leap of faith, she'd eased her foot off the button, written down her number, and slid the paper back to him. He'd given her a relieved wink, retreated meekly from the bank, and heaved a sigh of relief. The rest, as they say, was history.

Which was why he'd never had to work with numbers again, thank God, because he was terrible at math. And Valentina, who would handle their finances going forward, had gone on to become a successful business manager for a few small companies, and was currently the operations manager for the oldest church in their town, with many committees—as well as the congregation's pastor—answering to her. But through it all, she always maintained the kind, caring demeanor that made everyone love her, including his entire family and their daughter, Michelle, who had graduated with honors from college and was now a successful screenwriter in California, where she lived with her new husband.

Valentina's own life hadn't been so easy. She'd grown up moderately poor in Madrid and had emigrated to the States when she was nine years old (and not speaking a word of English) with her godparents, who were looking to make their fortune in America before moving back to Spain for what they hoped would be a comfortable retirement. As for Valentina's parents, they had stayed behind in Madrid to work out some marital problems—as Catholics, divorce was out of the question—and hopefully later join their daughter. Sadly, only Valentina's mother would eventually make it across the Atlantic, dying of breast cancer not long after Bobby came into the picture. Most of the time it was just Valentina and her godparents, one of them being her mother's older sister, who ruled with an iron hand. Valentina served as the dutiful niece who cooked, cleaned, did her schoolwork (gradually losing any trace of her European accent) and generally behaved herself. To say she was sheltered was an understatement; Bobby would be the first boy she'd date without a chaperone.

So when he'd taken her out that first time, for a drink at a fancy supper club, he was shocked that the girl, who personably dealt with customers every day at her job, barely said a word. He ended up having to carry the entire conversation, something he wasn't used to. Even the rose he'd brought her to begin the evening hadn't elicited much of a response (though she would later have it framed, with his bank deposit note, to be displayed forever on her bedroom dresser). When he'd dropped her off that night they'd shaken hands—quite unlike what had been going on the past few years when Bobby found himself waking up, in his apartment or other venues, next to a variety of girls, some of whose names escaped him in the early morning light. "Should I call you again?" he'd asked tentatively.

"Yes," she'd answered demurely. "I enjoy your company."

And that was it.

What he didn't know, and would find out much later, was that once the door closed behind her, Valentina's wizened mother had predicted, "You're going to marry that boy." It was too bad she hadn't lived to see it.

\* \* \*

He looked over at his wife as she tried to get into the romance novel she'd brought along for the plane ride, in case the movie choices were crappy. Valentina had matured gracefully despite a troublesome knee that had cut down on her daily exercise regimen, and she was an attractive fifty-six. In fact, at times both she and her husband were questioned by residents of their retirement communities as to whether they were actually owners. Overall, they were in a good place.

The Bermuda trip had actually been her idea. Now that they would be splitting time between their 55-and-older golf course complexes in Westchester and Florida, having sold their house after Michelle's departure, they could come and go as they pleased, with the church giving Val the luxury of working remotely. So, they'd jetted down to the Fort Lauderdale condo for a few weeks, and were now flying out of Miami to their favorite island destination for a couple more weeks of fun. The Romeros had traveled extensively in Europe during their marriage, with Spain a frequent location, since all of Valentina's relatives had, indeed, gone back there to retire after working hard in America for so many years. But Bermuda, where they'd spent their honeymoon and returned numerous times with and without Michelle, kept calling them back. They loved the relaxed atmosphere, the British influence, and the kindness of the natives. Yes, it was expensive as hell, considering virtually everything on the island had to be imported. But it was clean, safe, and picturesque. Valentina considered it their special place, which was surprising, since Bobby's first visit there had not been their honeymoon, but a spring break vacation the year after he'd graduated from college, the year of *The Disaster*.

# Chapter Two

"Ladies and gentlemen, welcome to Delta flight 622 from Miami to Bermuda," trilled the cheery male flight attendant. "Our flight time should be approximately two hours and thirty-five minutes. There have been some storms over the Atlantic that we'll have to keep an eye on, but the temperature in Bermuda is currently a balmy 86°. Please secure your seat belts, and return your seat to the upright position. Make sure any personal items are stowed beneath the seat in front of you. After a brief explanation of our safety and emergency procedures, we will lift off and you will have full Wi-Fi access and a choice of movies, TV programs or music. If you need to purchase headphones… "

Bobby sneaked a look at Valentina, who was decked out in a floral print sun dress, with aviator sunglasses perched atop her still-luxurious hair, kept dark with a little help from her hairdresser. Though they traveled a lot, his wife wasn't a big fan of flying (and his daughter had become terrified of it after 9/11). Valentina tried to maintain a calm demeanor, but upon takeoffs and landings she would unfailingly grip his hand on their shared armrest and hold tight until it was over. Conversely, Bobby had long since ceased to seriously listen to the safety reminders robotically distributed by the attendants. He simply eased back in his seat and pulled his Yankees ball cap over his eyes.

Getting comfortable on any prolonged flight wasn't easy for Bobby. The hip replacement over a year ago—his first surgery ever, at age 61, no less—had gone well, and he was still hitting the gym as religiously as before, with an elliptical trainer taking the place of early morning runs. Of course, he didn't look as good as during his football days in college, but he was pleased to see he presented well at his college team's reunions and the like. The fact that he still had most of his hair, though it was now flecked with gray, was a comfort as well. But there were some days where the hip or knees or back would bark at him, usually during a change in the weather—or air pressure, as he would shortly be experiencing. He couldn't wait to soak in the warm waters of Jobson's Cove on the South Shore of the island, close to the efficiency apartments near Astwood Park where he and Valentina usually stayed during their Bermudian sojourns.

"Prepare for takeoff. All crew members should be in their seats."

"We'll be there in no time," Bobby assured his wife, whose polished pink nails were digging into the palm of his hand nearly deep enough to draw blood.

"I know, it's just… "

"Ah, c'mon, Val," he moaned, "don't tell me you were watching one of those Discovery Channel shows on the Bermuda Triangle and got spooked—"

"It was the Travel Channel, Bobby, and you have to admit they can't solve some of that stuff, even after all these years."

"It's bullshit."

"Not to the people who disappeared on those boats and airplanes. Or their families."

Bobby sighed. "You need a rum Swizzle," he suggested, referring to Bermuda's famous party cocktail.

She allowed herself a chuckle. "Remember that night on our honeymoon?"

"Yeah," he said. "We did that evening glass-bottom boat cruise that included all the Swizzles you could drink, and you sure got your money's worth."

"Back at the hotel, we got into bed and I kept telling you to stop the boat. That was some night."

"It sure was. But the rest of the honeymoon was great."

"You know it." She leaned over and kissed him on the cheek, and he silently thanked God for her, and how she had saved him from *The Disaster*, which had, ironically, started to germinate on the very island to which he was now headed.

\* \* \*

Her name was Lucy Spencer, a.k.a. *The Disaster.* For the past 30-plus years he couldn't even bring himself to utter her name. But in 1979, she was the love of his life. His dream girl.

They had met in college when they'd taken the same class during the first semester of his junior year. He'd looked across the room and *BAM.* She was doing something like flipping her blonde, Farrah Fawcett locks out of her piercing blue eyes, wearing a sheer sweater or some such garment that revealed a curvaceous body, and he was hooked. Bobby had had girlfriends in high school and had dated here and there in college, but active pursuit wasn't in his DNA. For one thing, despite his "Joe Jock" buddies aggressively enjoying the live-for-today, disco era lifestyle, Bobby tended to hang back and let things come to him. Besides, he could be charming to the opposite sex in his own understated way, and was at heart a hopeless romantic (his teammates sometimes jokingly called him "Bobby Romeo") who truly believed—at least at this stage in his life—that real love was akin to a Beatles ballad like "If I Fell" or "And I Love Her." He knew better, but there was a part of him that wanted to believe that love, or romance, equated to candlelit dinners and long walks on the beach, especially if they were with someone as alluring as Lucy Spencer. And so, he went after her with a passion usually reserved for his off-season training program. As a running back he was described as tenacious, a guy who didn't go down easily and kept fighting for every yard. He simply transferred that attitude to the pursuit of Lucy.

It hadn't been easy at first. Lucy's wasp-y heritage seemed at odds with Bobby's Italian sensibilities, and his own parents, who had always wanted him to marry a "nice Italian girl," had their reservations. Even his maternal grandmother, whom he adored, had warned, "Watch out, Bobby. These people, they're not like us. They're very cold." Of course, Grandma's cultural bias reflected the mores of another era, but he could, at times, see in Lucy indications of the old woman's description. This girl wasn't one to show a lot of feeling in public. After a few dates, once they'd become "an item," they would hold hands and such, but outside of the occasional peck on the cheek, it was all pretty reserved. And though Bobby wasn't really an exhibitionist like some of his buddies (and former girlfriends, for that matter) he did think about her lack of warmth occasionally. But then he'd dismiss it with the disclaimer that once they'd officially made love, in the upstairs bedroom at a junior year football party, he was quite content with the arrangement.

There were some bumps in the road, however. One that did nag did him was their first Christmas together. They were alone for a minute at his family's house after just exchanging gifts, and he had said, sincerely, "I love you, Lucy," almost expecting a crescendo of violin (or Beatles) music to materialize. But her reaction was almost one of surprise, and though she kissed him, she never did return the sentiment verbally. Again, in his ardor for her he tossed it off.

At the end of their junior year, things seemed to deepen, and despite summer jobs that took them in opposite directions, the couple made the one hour drive to each other's houses frequently. Their dates were fun and the sex—whenever possible—was exciting and new. Bobby always prided himself on being a patient, giving lover, and Lucy, though not as demonstrative as women he would encounter later (including his wife) was a compliant partner. In addition, and perhaps more importantly, Lucy's parents clearly liked Bobby, as did her younger sister, with whom Lucy was constantly at odds. He frequently found himself in the role of buffer between the two siblings, who were very different in personality. Lucy was the conservative, levelheaded one, while Amy was the wild child who didn't take most things seriously. As for Bobby's parents, they gradually warmed to Lucy, especially when they saw how deeply their eldest son cared for her. Bobby's younger brother by two years, whose name was Joe, simply thought she was hot, while his kid sister Paula, five years his junior, looked to her for the guidance an older sister would have provided. And Lucy happily obliged.

As a traditional Italian family, such modern concepts as divorce were virtually unheard of. By the time he'd met Lucy, Bobby's parents had been happily married for twenty years and were still going strong. Lucy's family life was just as stable, though her parents were a bit more liberal in their way of thinking. Bobby had every reason, then, to think this was the natural order of things, one that he and Lucy could easily follow.

By the time Bobby's senior football season—a rousing success for him personally and for his undefeated team—had ended, it was understood that the couple had a solid relationship, so much so that their peers came to them with their problems. And so, when they went away for a long weekend the following summer with one of Bobby's teammates and his girlfriend to Martha's Vineyard, nary an eyebrow was raised. Their future together seemed assured.

Graduation had signaled the end of the first phase of their relationship, but Bobby was already looking forward. He landed his first teaching job and smoothly transitioned into his new career, while Lucy made use of her political science degree by going into prelaw. It was natural, then, that he would think the upcoming Christmas holiday would be the perfect time to ask the girl of his dreams to marry him. When he told his parents of the plan there were some raised eyebrows. His dad, the pragmatic one, asked if he felt financially ready to take the plunge while living at home and earning a modest private school salary. His mom simply said, "Are you sure about this, Bobby? This is a big step." When he assured her he'd thought it out, she came around to the idea and even helped him pick out Lucy's ring. Now all he had to do was pop the question. He was nearing the goal line.

And so, after doing the noble thing and asking her parents—who gave their blessing—he set up the big event for his house on Christmas Eve, when the rest of his family would be next-door at a neighborhood party. A fire was crackling in the living room, and Lucy turned up on this frigid night with her cheeks rosy from the cold, the dusting of freckles on her fair skin standing out. They had a glass of wine, he put on a Beatles album, waited for "And I Love Her," took out the rock, and popped the question.

Her mouth fell open. She didn't answer.

Bobby felt like he'd run into a pileup on the 1 yard line. He had to bounce off and find daylight somehow. "Are you all right?" he asked.

"Y-yes," she'd replied. "I just… didn't expect it so soon—"

*So soon?* he thought, trying not to betray his panic. *It's been two freaking years!* He was crushed. "Well," he managed, "I had thought—"

"Yes," she whispered.

"Yes, you'll marry me?" he said hopefully.

"Yes, Bobby."

Relief washed over him in such a wave that he almost passed out. "Want me to put the ring on?"

"Sure," she said, holding out her hand, which was trembling.

*Please fit, please fit*, he thought. *This has been hard enough.*

The ring fit. They kissed. Bobby and Lucy were engaged, hallelujah.

Subsequent weeks were spent making announcements and the like, and formulating preliminary plans. It was agreed that the wedding would take place during the summer a year and a half hence, to allow time for both of them, who were still living at home, to save up some money. Their friends were thrilled, and their families began to socialize more frequently, after an engagement party Lucy's parents threw at her father's yacht club.

Halfway through the festivities that day, the couple excused themselves and walked out on the dock that overlooked Long Island Sound. "Are you happy, Lucy?" Bobby asked.

"Yes, of course," she answered.

"Excited?"

"Yeah," she said. "It's all so crazy."

"How so?"

"I don't know," she said. "It's like, one day you're just... engaged, and everything changes."

"But, for the better, right?"

She nodded, and kissed him.

## Chapter Three

The Bermuda trip of '79 came about after Bobby had heard about the island from college teammates who'd done spring break there, while it seemed the rest of the world—including him—was in Daytona Beach or Ft. Lauderdale drinking beer and going wild. According to them, Bermuda was quieter, more refined, and tailor-made for a romantic guy like himself. He'd outgrown the Florida craziness, anyway. So, when he pitched the idea to Lucy, she'd agreed immediately. "Why don't you ask Barnes and his girlfriend to join us?" she suggested. "We could kind of split the bills there. I've heard it's on the pricey side."

"Sure, if that's okay with you," he said. "We'll get separate rooms, though, right?"

"Of course, silly," she said with a smile that filled his heart and made him amorous at the same time.

So they had gone to Bermuda with his best buddy, Barnes Nevin, and his girlfriend Tish and enjoyed a relaxing, fun-filled week of sightseeing, eating, drinking, and lovemaking. Barnes had to go back a day earlier because of his job, with Tish in tow, but they'd nevertheless had a great time.

Or so Bobby thought. Because after that, there were subtle shifts in his relationship with Lucy that he either disregarded or failed to pick up on. "Stupid stuff," he usually said to himself dismissively. But in the following autumn, as football season was drawing to a close, it all came crashing down with a blindside hit worse than any linebacker had ever laid on him.

Lucy had just started a new job as a legal assistant at a prestigious law office in White Plains, the largest city in Westchester County, which promised to bring in more income for the couple. Bobby was exhausted, as usual, after the football season ended, but looked forward to the upcoming holidays. It was on a date at their favorite Mexican restaurant that Lucy, between the guacamole and chips and the main course, dropped the bomb.

"I want to postpone the wedding," she said abruptly.

"What?"

"Postpone the wedding. I want to put it off for a while."

Bobby stared at her. "But it's…like seven months away," he stammered. "Put it off till when?"

"I don't know," she whispered.

"*Why?*"

"I don't know," she repeated.

Bobby almost threw up. This was beyond his comprehension. A flood of embarrassment, powerlessness—and, finally, rage—came over him. It was out of his mouth before he could stop it. "Give me the ring," he said, biting off the words.

"But—"

"Give… me… the… ring," he repeated.

She slipped it off and handed it to him. He stood up and pocketed it. "We're going," he said tonelessly. He took out a twenty for the chips and sangria and dropped it on the table. They walked to his car as if in a trance. He opened the passenger door for her, let her get in, and tried mightily not to slam it. Then he drove her home, an agonizingly silent half hour ride. Once there, she looked at him for a second, her eyes misty, and got out, gently closing the Firebird's door behind her. He sat there, his eyes following her up the path to the front door, willing her to turn around and come running back to him, apologizing for her stupidity, for ruining both their lives. But instead she slipped inside, her back to him. The light over the door went out.

He never saw her again.

\* \* \*

The next few weeks were surrealistic for Bobby, from the drive home that night—during which he'd cried the whole way—to the outrage from his mother ("How *dare* she? It just proves you're too good for her"). Thankfully, she stopped just short of quoting his grandmother about "those people." Next up were the stunned friends and relatives whom he had to face. As for his former fiancée, she appeared to have sequestered herself in her house till things blew over, while he dragged himself to work every day and tried to get through it. He seemed to be acting out a version of a poem he was teaching at school, "The Rime of the Ancient Mariner," where this poor schmuck is punished for a crime he committed by having to travel through time retelling his tale. When Bobby explained what had happened over and over, his story was met with a mixture of incredulity and pity, which made him feel even worse.

He did speak to her on the phone once—after all, there was a joint bank account they'd established to liquidate, and engagement gifts they'd been given to divvy up—but she seemed disinterested. "You can take it all," she said woodenly. Bobby wouldn't have it. He made a list of who'd given them what, had Barnes drop off her side of the gifts at her house (being a loyal buddy, he'd wanted to just throw the stuff on her front lawn, but Bobby made him promise to place it near the front door and leave) and sent her a check for the bank account cash. And then it was *really* over, on December 19, 1979.

Merry Christmas, Bobby. Welcome to *The Disaster*.

* * *

The following few years were a blur, with Bobby's teaching and coaching careers thrust to the forefront to fill the void left by the breakup. And though for awhile the first year his heart skipped a beat every time the phone rang or the mail came, deep down he knew a reunion was unlikely. He became alternately sad, depressed, angry and cold. His family welcomed his decision to move to his own apartment, as he seemed irritable and distant on the best of days. Despite his never seeming to be lacking for female companionship, Bobby's cynical outlook had led to a brick-by-brick construction of an emotional fortress, one so strong that not even the sweetest—or hottest—girls could find a way into. Even by his own standards, Bobby had become an asshole. "You've got to snap out of this," his mother admonished during one family gathering. "The only time you're even approachable is when you've had a few drinks." Oh yeah, there was that, too.

Bobby had never been a teetotaler. Beer consumption had come naturally to him in his high school days as a part of the jock culture he was immersed in, and it had continued through college. But now it was taking a couple double shots of Jameson's or Johnny Walker to dull the pain, or at least make him sociable on the weekends when he frequented local bars or hung out with Barnes or some of his other college buddies. And then there were other times when he just poured himself a strong one from his bachelor pad's liquor cabinet and put on music, staring at the ceiling. His favorite tunes were the current sad ones, like Bob Seger's "Main Street" and Joe Jackson's "Breaking Us In Two." Even his Beatle tastes changed, from the romantic optimism of the early Mop Top songs he'd lived by, to his depressing album of choice, *Rubber Soul*. He listened to it, over and over. And when songs like "I'm Looking Through You," "Think For Yourself," and "Girl," John Lennon's lament over a broken love, started to play, he'd sigh and take another sip. (In fact, he'd never quite get that album out of his system, naming his only daughter Michelle, the title of another melancholy track). At times he'd wonder what *she* was doing, whether she was thinking about him, or if she'd even been affected by the heartache she had wrought. This would lead to him second-guessing himself, wondering if he'd acted too rashly on that fateful night in the Mexican restaurant.

And he would take another sip.

\* \* \*

By the time Valentina came into his life, *The Disaster* was like a dormant parasite that would occasionally resurface, only to be held in check by the love and understanding of this extraordinary girl. Gradually, his protective wall cracked as he allowed himself, in small increments, to trust her. Any fear of commitment he still harbored was squashed down, but not without effort. And when they were married, he couldn't have been more happy, nor his family and friends. Of course, Barnes, by then on his second wife, was in the wedding party. But it was an unmentioned understanding between him and his lifelong buddy— as well as all his relatives and acquaintances—that *The Disaster* was never to be mentioned again. It was as if she'd fallen off the face of the earth, like she'd never existed.

All things considered, it was incredible that Bobby and his former fiancée had never crossed paths in subsequent years. Which was odd, because they both lived in the same area of the same county (as did Valentina) for nearly the next four decades. Only Bobby's sister had seen her once, maybe five years after the breakup, in a restaurant, and had given her the evil eye until she left.

Then, of course, social media had been created, and though Bobby wasn't the most tech-savvy guy around, he did find himself Googling her one day in the early 2000s. And there she was, under Lucy Spencer-Wisniewski, living upcounty and still looking pretty good, her hair a little shorter, the figure filled out a bit more, with a tall, grayish husband and a

19

couple blonde haired kids who were in high school at the time. (He allowed himself a petty moment to say to the husband, "Yeah, buddy, smile all you want, but I got there first.") Anyway, in the Facebook family portrait she looked happy. He clicked off, hoping this would put everything to rest, especially the dreams.

For the life of him, Bobby couldn't understand why, some forty years later, *The Disaster* popped up every month or so while he slept. And the dreams always followed the same script, more or less: he is his current age, or something close, and unattached apparently, as both Val and Michelle never appear. He makes the drive over to *The Disaster's* old house, where her parents, who look older, still reside. It is understood that she has been married, and has kids—perhaps she's estranged from her husband—it's never completely clear. What does happen, however, is that Bobby, after having to wait an uncomfortable amount of time with his almost in-laws, sees *The Disaster's* car pull into the driveway. She gets out, comes inside, greets her parents, and then goes off somewhere with Bobby, perhaps the backyard, to talk. She looks at him with the same misty eyes he'd beheld that night so long ago. And then, without fail, *without freaking fail*, he asks her the same question: "*Why?*"

And that's how it would end. His eyes would snap open, and he'd realize he was in bed with the woman he would happily be with forever.

But still…

# Chapter Four

Bobby had managed to doze off but was awakened, as usual, by an obnoxious little kid sitting behind him on the plane who was alternately kicking his seat back and whining to her mother about being bored. "Just watch *Finding Nemo*," cooed the overwrought parent.

"I've already seen it like a hundred times!" screeched the brat.

"Your tone of voice is really not appropriate," said the mother, as if that would really shut the kid up. Val looked over at him and rolled her eyes. Michelle would *never* have behaved like that. Usually, her nose was buried in a book on flights and in restaurants, in those pre-iPhone days.

So, Bobby went to his go-to set of padded headphones and flipped on the MLB Network for highlights of the previous night's game. His beloved Yankees, led by young Aaron Judge, had beaten the Blue Jays and were making a late-season push to try to catch the Red Sox for the AL East Division lead. It didn't seem likely, though they were still going to win close to 100 games and make the playoffs. But as he stared into the seat back monitor before him, he suddenly felt a tremor, then a kind of grinding sensation.

Valentina removed her own headphones and gave him a concerned look. "You feel that?" she said.

"Yeah," he answered, staying calm. "Don't sweat it, Val, it's probably just some turbulence from the storms they told us about."

"But that felt like *inside* the plane," she said, her voice wavering a bit.

She wasn't the only one who was concerned, apparently. Upon removing his headset Bobby could hear murmuring all over the place. Then the voice of the pilot, cool as a cucumber, came over the intercom:

"Ladies and gentlemen, we are experiencing some mechanical difficulties and will be diverting to the Charlotte Airport to check it out. We should be over land in a matter of—"

*BANG!*

It felt as if something had torn loose in the belly of the plane, and people started screaming. "I'm scared! I'm scared!" wailed the little girl behind Bobby.

"We're going down!" bellowed a stout man across the aisle from Val, who had turned white.

The plane seemed to shake, and then sharply banked. Food and drinks flew off snack trays as passengers groped for their seatbelts. Then the oxygen masks dropped from the ceiling. It was all happening so quickly.

Bobby turned to his wife, who had again dug her nails into his hand, her nostrils dilated, those Spanish eyes wide with terror. "I love you," she said.

He never got a chance to respond, as the world went black.

* * *

He came to, slowly, wedged back in his seat, his hands gripping the armrests. As his eyes fluttered open he gave thanks for not being dead, but immediately noticed something amiss. The TV monitor playing the MLB Network in the seat before him was gone, in its place material of a hideous paisley pattern. Gingerly he lifted his left hand to the side of his head, feeling for blood, then pulled it back sharply. The headphones were gone, as was his Yankees ball cap. Had they flown off? But wait—he'd felt *something* over his ear. He brought his fingers up again. It was hair. Lots of it.

"Bobby? Bobby?" called a voice that seemed to be coming from deep inside a well. Then once more, and clear in his right ear: *"Bobby!"*

He turned and looked into the sky-blue eyes of Lucy Spencer.

* * *

"My man, I think you passed out when we hit that air pocket," said Barnes, who was holding a half empty plastic cup of beer as he leaned in over Lucy's shoulder. "Are you okay? You want me to call a stewardess?"

He looked at his best buddy, whose blonde hair, parted in the middle and layered over his ears, contained not a hint of gray. "Nah, Barnes, I'm okay," he managed, but he truly was not.

"You want a glass of water?" asked Lucy, concern in those blue eyes. "I can get you one."

He thought, *What the hell do you care if I'm okay?* But instead he said, "That would be nice, Lulu,"

23

and realized it was the first time he'd uttered her nickname in forty years. Barnes returned to his seat, where Tish gave Bobby a supportive wave. Bobby watched Lucy, who was wearing a tank top, cut-off jean shorts and clogs, wiggle out of her seat and head off down the aisle, her shapely backside swaying. His heart was pounding.

Slowly, Bobby rose from his seat and looked around for Valentina, who was nowhere to be seen. Instead, the paisley seats were occupied by older gents in knit shirts and plaid pants, middle-aged women with lacquered hair, and younger people such as himself with either disco era silk shirts, gold necklaces and bellbottoms, or hippie-style tee shirts and patchwork jeans. Most of the girls had either the shorter Dorothy Hamill layer cut or, like Lucy, the Farrah Fawcett hairdo. There wasn't a cell phone to be seen. It was bizarre.

Bobby eased back down into his seat and collected himself. *Okay, don't panic*, he thought. *Slow down your breathing, dammit! Here's what's happening. You're having the mother of all Disaster dreams. In a little while you'll wake up and Val will be there and it'll be just another day. So calm down and roll with it.*

"Here's your water," said Lucy, handing him a plastic cup. "You probably shouldn't have had those beers in the airport bar. I swear, every time you and Barnes get together, you guys are like little kids."

"Yeah," he responded meekly. "Sorry."

"It's okay," she said, and kissed him on the forehead. He inhaled the fragrance of her favorite perfume, L'air du Temps, which he hadn't experienced in years. It made him lightheaded all over again. "We should be touching down in Bermuda soon," she said brightly. "I can't wait."

"Me neither. But, uh, I think I have to use the bathroom now."

"No problem," she said, and leaned back into her seat to let him by. He shuffled slowly to the rear of the plane, grabbing on to every seat top for support as he went, examining the passengers as if they were aliens. One girl who looked about eighteen, with way too much mascara and a tube top, gave him a wink and a wave. *Jeez, she's young enough to be my daughter*, he thought.

Once inside the lavatory he closed his eyes and exhaled, but turning to the sink to wash his face gave him a start. The person peering back at him in the mirror was a stranger. All the gray was gone from his hair, which was lush and brown and covered his ears, tapering down his neck and barely missing his shoulders. His face was uncreased and his skin was tight, though in need of a good Bermuda tan.

He was wearing the orange tee shirt he'd bought a few years before when he and Barnes had gone to decrepit Roosevelt Stadium in Jersey City to see the Beach Boys and The Eagles together. *I wonder whatever became of that shirt?* he thought. *Tell you what, though. My arms really looked pumped.* And he had on his favorite faded jeans and Puma sneakers. Overall, a nice look. No wonder the babe had waved at him.

He remembered how it had been his first year teaching high school in the Bronx. The school was co-ed, and as a young football coach on a predominantly older, female staff, he had become somewhat of a heartthrob to the teenage girls, especially the seniors, who were given the option of wearing dresses instead of the mandatory Plain Jane uniforms of the underclassmen, and always dressed to impress. Some of the Hispanic girls, especially, were knockouts who looked like they were in their 20s. But Bobby, who was totally focused on being a successful teacher and coach, had been professional at all times; and besides, he'd had a girlfriend at the time who was a knockout herself.

He leaned over the cramped sink and washed his face, feeling a sting of pain in his left shoulder. *Ouch! What was that about?* And then he remembered: the slight shoulder separation he'd suffered against Fordham University midway during his senior season had taken a couple years to completely heal. But his hip felt fine. Then, as if he needed any more confirmation that this was a dream, he unzipped his jeans and pulled them down a bit. The 8" vertical scar on his leg from the hip surgery was gone.

Fearing that he had dallied too long, Bobby exited the restroom and made his way back to Lucy, who was reading *People Magazine*, its cover graced by a young Robin Williams. "Everything okay?" she asked sweetly as he squeezed by.

"Couldn't be better," he replied.

"So, what do you want to do first when we get there?" she asked.

He found himself unable to control the smirk that crossed his face.

"*Besides* that," she chided, giving him a light smack on the hand.

And then, as if he'd memorized the words from a script, he recited the following monologue: "Well, close by the airport there's supposed to be this cool bar called the Swizzle Inn. I figure we could take a taxi there from the airport, have a 'welcome to Bermuda' cocktail, and then take another taxi to the hotel."

"Sounds like fun. But what's a Swizzle? Is it a drink or something?"

Bobby well knew that a Bermuda rum Swizzle was comprised of dark and light spirits, fruit juices, Grenadine, falernum and Angostura bitters; in fact, he'd often whip up a batch at home with Val to share on their deck during the hot summer months. But again, he found himself saying, "I don't know, but we'll find out."

They called Barnes and Tish over and shared the plan, prompting memories of his best buddy's then-girlfriend to come back to him. He'd never liked Tish because she smoked too much, and not only cigarettes. And she had an airheaded way about her that tended to grate on his nerves. Barnes would himself tire of her in another year and end up marrying wife number one, a union that would end in an annulment. As for Lucy, she seemed to get along with Barnes's girlfriend just fine, but that didn't stop her from taking the occasional verbal swipe at Tish behind her back. Maybe because, like all of Barnes's girlfriends in those days, she was more than a little good-looking, and Lucy could be a touch catty if the other girl was a showoff, which Tish Riordan most certainly was.

Within minutes the captain made the announcement to prepare for landing. The stewardesses scurried up the aisles checking seat backs (Bobby had forgotten how cute they all used to be) and then buckled into their own stations. They drifted in smooth as silk, Bermuda's turquoise waters and palm trees visible from the windows, as was the nearby Swizzle Inn, in whose parking lot were stationed a number of motor scooters, the only kind of vehicle available for tourist hire. Bobby kept waiting for the dream to end, but the next thing he knew Lucy had popped out of her seat and was reaching for the overhead storage bin, the bottom of her tank top riding up over her flat stomach, her breasts full, and an old warm feeling stirred inside him. If this really was a dream, he wouldn't mind it going a bit longer.

# Chapter Five

"You're *sure* you want to make a stop-off before we hit the hotel?" asked Barnes suggestively as he walked alongside Bobby on the hot tarmac to the small Bermuda Airport terminal, the girls trailing behind.

"Calm down, son," he replied, "it's only like 11 AM in the morning. We've got the whole day ahead of us."

"You've gotta admit, though, the ladies are looking incredibly fine today."

"That they are," said Robbie, thinking, *Jeez, Barnes, if you thought more with the head on your shoulders, you wouldn't be a 3-time loser.* But he felt this wasn't the time to clue in his best friend about what the future would bring; in fact, he wondered if he even had the power to do so. It seemed that every time he opened his mouth, what came out was pre-programmed. So he kept his mouth shut and continued walking.

The terminal was small and hot, featuring a large wall portrait of Queen Elizabeth, looking much younger than the frail older woman in the extravagant hats and matching coats that he'd seen lately. Here, she appeared to be about forty, sporting the Royal bling, scepter and all. On another wall there hung a huge mounted sailfish. There were no metal detectors, only a couple of smartly uniformed attendants who were randomly checking bags.

Bobby had automatically started reaching for his belt when a look from Lucy that said *What on earth are you doing?* stopped him cold. This was the pre-9/11 world, after all.

"Are you here for business or pleasure?" politely asked the customs officer as Bobby proffered his passport.

Barnes, who was standing next to him, jerked his head back over his shoulder to where the girls stood chatting. "Are you kidding?" he replied, and even the staid black man had to crack a smile as he stamped their booklets.

"Well, in that case, carry on, gentlemen," he said, handing them back the passports.

After what seemed like an interminable amount of time, the luggage carousel kicked into gear, and the foursome gathered at the rail to retrieve their bags. Bobby knew that by the time he would return with his wife in the mid-80s, the facility would be technologically upgraded, and considerably more comfortable temperature-wise, but that was of no help in the sticky humidity of today.

"Boy, am I thirsty," said Tish, her usual lament.

Bobby's adult mind suggested he tell her to make sure she keep hydrated with copious amounts of water, but he inexplicably said, "Yeah, I could use a couple cocktails myself."

Finally their bags came through the plastic flaps onto the conveyor belt, and the guys scooped them up quickly. Bobby had forgotten what his luggage looked like back then and momentarily panicked, but found himself mechanically reaching for a blue hard-sided suitcase with a red ribbon tied to the handle. Of course; he'd borrowed his dad's luggage for the trip. This was before soft-sided bags with wheels came into vogue, so when he hefted it he grunted with the effort. Lucy's suitcase was even heavier. "What have you got in there, Lulu?" he cracked.

"Never you mind," she replied innocently.

Outside, they hailed a cab from the taxi stand. All the cars in the queue were compacts, as neither the SUV nor its predecessor, the minivan, had been introduced. There were a couple Volkswagen micro buses, however. The driver, a dark-skinned man with an Afro and a pleasant Bermudian accent, wedged their luggage into the Toyota's trunk as they squeezed into the back seat. The car had no air-conditioning, so the windows were rolled down. "Where to, folks?" he asked.

"The Swizzle Inn, please," said Bobby.

"Righto, an excellent place to begin!" he replied, and they were off. They crossed the causeway that connected the airport to the island, their driver patiently giving way to other cars and scooters. "Is this your first visit to Bermuda?" he asked over his shoulder.

"Yes," said Bobby, thinking *Nope*.

"It's beautiful," offered Tish.

"Thank you, Miss. We're very proud of it. Hopefully this will be the first of numerous visits for all of you."

*You've got no idea, buddy*, thought Bobby, who would be back many times in subsequent years, including his "current" trip with Val.

As the palm trees, bougainvillea and hibiscus flowers whizzed by, Bobby took in the familiar sites of pastel-covered houses with whitewashed tile roofs that dotted the landscape, a style that so enamored he and

Val that they had purchased prints of these dwellings by local artists on their honeymoon and had them matted and framed for display in their den.

The taxi pulled into the parking lot of the Swizzle Inn, which as noon time approached was already packed with motor scooters. Revelers sat at tables inside or upstairs on the bar's balcony. Barnes said, "I got this, Bob," and paid the cabbie in American dollars, which was as readily accepted as Bermudian money. However, his buddy's magnanimous gesture got him to thinking about his own wallet, which provided a noticeable bulge in his back pocket. He made a mental note to check it out in the men's room once they got seated.

They found a table indoors tucked away in a cool corner and set their bags down. An Afro-Bermudian server immediately appeared, attired in a Swizzle Inn tee shirt and Bermuda shorts. "And what can I provide you fine people this day?" she piped.

"I'd like to try those Swizzles we've heard so much about," said Lucy.

"That's our most popular drink, obviously," she replied. "But we also make a fantastic Dark and Stormy."

"What's that?" asked Barnes.

*Barritt's ginger beer, Gosling's rum, and lime, served over ice in a tall glass*, thought Bobby, who'd actually included this concoction in his summer rotation back home.

The server recited the ingredients to the four, but only Bobby opted to try it for the first round, as he'd always found Swizzles a bit sweet for his taste. Once their order was placed, he excused himself to go to the restroom. He entered a toilet stall, latched the door behind him, and pulled out his battered wallet. Inside were his driver's license which listed his childhood home's address, $300 in cash, and another couple hundred in American Express travelers checks, which he hadn't used in years. Gone were his photos of Valentina and Michelle, and his AAA and AARP cards. In fact, there were no credit cards at all, only the card for his medical insurance that he'd obtained through the school where he taught. He made a mental note to watch his pennies, recalling that he and Lucy had run low on cash near the end of this trip, despite her bringing more in travelers checks than he had.

He washed his hands, again looking in the mirror at himself, the visage not as jarring as on the plane. But still, his head was spinning from the difficulty of living in two time periods, at least in his mind. Apparently, he could only act in the present of 1979; otherwise, some force would prevent him. However, he determined that he had to let this play out as long as the dream (?) lasted, if only to get a handle on just what had gone wrong between himself and Lucy during the trip. But, boy, this had to be the most realistic *Disaster* dream he'd ever had. Was it something he'd eaten that morning in the Starbucks at Miami International?

Back at the table, the party was in full swing, with his friends already half done with their opening round of drinks. He took his first sip of a Dark and Stormy, the combination of tangy, ice cold ginger beer and rum sliding down his throat. "Delicious," he declared. "I could get used to this."

"The Swizzles are great, too," said Lucy. "Like Hawaiian Punch or something. But the waitress warned us that they kind of sneak up on you." Bobby remembered Val on the glass- bottom boat and smiled.

*Let's see*, he thought, *how old would she be now, in 1979? She's five years younger than me... Christ, she's only seventeen right now, still in high school, living in that three-family house in Yonkers with her godparents.*

"Hey, man, you notice how everyone's posted their business cards or written their names on the walls?" asked Barnes, breaking his reverie. "We've gotta get our numbers up there, Bobby," he said, referring to the football jersey numbers they'd worn in both high school and college.

"Sure thing," said Bobby. "Anyone got a—" he tried to say Sharpie, but of course they hadn't been invented yet, so what came out was, "Magic Marker."

"Nope," said the girls in unison. But the waitress, who had just drifted over for a second round order, lent the boys a black ballpoint pen. Soon Barnes and Bobby were inscribing their names into a nearby wooden post, a semi-carving that would still be visible upon Bobby's honeymoon seven years later: *#32 and #21 wuz here!*

"Will you two ever grow up?" cracked Tish as she sucked on the ice from her empty glass.

They decided the second round would be their last and would then press on to the hotel they'd booked months ago on the recommendation of one of Bobby's teammates: the Reefside Apartments on the South Shore. After splitting the bill and hailing a taxi, they pushed off on the winding, twenty-five minute ride towards the picturesque beaches of Warwick Parish, passing through small settlements before entering the Bermudian capital city of Hamilton with its many shops, restaurants, bars, and boats in the marina, where a couple cruise ships rocked gently at their moorings. Then they climbed to the South Road and the cliffs that bordered that part of the island, towards the famous Gibbs Hill lighthouse and various small hotels and tourist apartments. They passed the only convenience store on the South Road (where the prices, even for a bag of chips, were exorbitant) and drifted by the Astwood Cove Apartments where Bobby, Val and Michelle usually stayed on their vacations. Memories of all these places came back in a sensory overload that made him close his eyes.

"You okay?" asked Lucy.

"Oh, yeah. The waitress was right about those tropical drinks sneaking up on you."

"Finally!" declared Barnes as their taxi eased into the tidy parking lot of the low-slung suite of bungalows that looked out over the cliffs and the surrounding Atlantic Ocean. Palm trees and bougainvillea framed the pink cottages which, according to the travel brochure, were equipped with functioning kitchenettes.

"Wow," said Tish as they emerged from the taxi. Bobby dug into his pocket and paid the driver, who set their bags by the office entrance. They entered the lobby, which featured exotic potted plants and teak furniture with floral pattern cushions.

"Can I help you?" asked the smiling desk clerk, a fair-skinned Bermudian girl.

Again, Bobby was gripped by momentary panic. Had they registered as married couples, or the guys and girls separately? Barnes rescued him when he nonchalantly announced, "We're the Nevins and the Romeros."

"Ah, yes, here you are. Your rooms are prepaid, so all I have to do is inform you that although there is a phone in each of your units, the rates are rather pricey for a call to the States. The pool and bar can be accessed from the back door of your bungalows, and there's a staircase down the cliffside to the beach below. Please be sure to have some kind of footwear on when you plan to descend, as the wooden steps can become a little slippery, especially after a rain shower, which can occur at any time here on the island. Please utilize the hand railings for safety's sake, and I wouldn't recommend navigating them after a few rum Swizzles." She allowed herself a brief wink, then handed over the keys to Bobby and Barnes. "My name is Joyce. Please let me know if you need anything, and I hope you'll enjoy your stay with us."

"I'm sure we will," said Bobby.

They picked up their bags and left the office, bearing to the right, in search of the last two bungalows that comprised the hotel. "What should we do this afternoon?" said Barnes.

"Well, the first thing should be to rent our scooters. The hotel brochure said they have a shuttle to take us to the rental place," offered Lucy.

"Sounds great," said Barnes. "Why don't we meet here in an hour. That'll give us time to... unpack." He wiggled his eyebrows mischievously while Tish rolled her eyes.

As Bobby turned toward the door of the bungalow he'd share with his fiancée, he realized he was incredibly excited—and terrified—at the same time.

"You having trouble?" asked Lucy as he fumbled with the key.

*Not yet,* he thought.

# Chapter Six

Both in high school and college, Bobby had returned kickoffs for his football team, a task not for the faint of heart, as the prospect of bringing the ball upfield as eleven defenders tore downfield at breakneck speed to destroy you was undesirable to most of his teammates. But Bobby was quite good at it, though he'd never taken one all the way.

What Bobby especially enjoyed, however, was the sense of anticipation and exhilaration—mixed with a touch of fear—he experienced as he waited on the goal line for the referee to blow his whistle so the opposing kicker could let it fly. On a cool October night or afternoon with the crowd standing and his teammates jumping up and down at their positions, eagerly awaiting that first hit, there was no place he'd rather be. And ever since the last kickoff return of his senior year, he'd been trying to find that feeling again in a variety of diversions, all of which fell short.

Until now.

He brought their suitcases straight to the bedroom of the bungalow, which was comfortably appointed with rattan furniture and Bermudian seascape paintings on its teal walls. The bed was a four-poster double, smaller than the queen he and Val enjoyed at both their condos. A pineapple motif was carved into the tan wood headboard.

"Nice place," said Bobby, his heart triphammering.

"It'll do," Lucy said with a smile. She sat on the edge of the mattress and patted the spot next to her.

Of all Bobby Romero's good qualities, loyalty was his most valued (and probably the strongest one he shared with Barnes, which was why they were so close), so as he sat down next to Lucy, his mind spun with the implications of what was about to happen. He hadn't been with another woman for almost 35 years, since he'd gotten serious with Valentina. Not that there hadn't been opportunities that had come along here and there, opportunities that he'd quickly dismissed after weighing what they would provide against the rock-solid certainty of his wife's unconditional love. But then again, this was 1979.

"Were finally here," he said, struggling for words. He looked deeply into those eyes that would seem so lifeless and cold only months later, searching for some kind of clue, *anything*, that would indicate the impending dissipation of her affection for him, but there was none. She leaned in and kissed him sweetly on the mouth, first brushing his lips, and then going in more deeply, her eyes closed. He deftly brought his hand from her shoulder to her full, firm breast, and gently squeezed.

"Love me, Bobby," she purred, the old signal that things were underway. Within seconds they had shed their clothes, the overhead ceiling fan faintly caressing their skin. Making love to Lucy Spencer was a pleasure. She was so young and beautiful and supple that he found himself totally lost in the long-forgotten essence of her, from the smell of that L'air du Temps to the thickness of her hair and softness of her skin. And to her credit, Lucy seemed totally lost in Bobby as well. But underneath it all, like a bubble rising from the deepest Arctic well, there came to his brain the image of Valentina's face, those big brown eyes questioning—

"Uh, Bobby? Aren't you forgetting something?" Lucy said in a half moan as he slid on top of her.

He pulled back, momentarily alarmed. Of course. He wasn't wearing a condom, and Lucy would not start using the pill until that summer. He mumbled, "Oops, sorry," slipped off her and opened the latches on his suitcase, praying they would be there. And they were, tucked inside the front of one of his Topsider moccasins, where he always stowed valuable items while traveling. *Thank you God*, he thought. He fumbled with the wrapper and she chuckled. "Gee, Bobby, it's like you've never done this before."

*No, but it's been a long time*, he thought as he finally slipped it on. And so, they continued where they'd left off, with Lucy moaning his name and Bobby thinking, *Oh Val, I'm so sorry, so sorry, so sorry.*

\* \* \*

Minutes later he lay back and gazed at her. She had primly pulled the covers over her breasts despite their somewhat sweaty encounter and blew her bangs upward out of her eyes. Her pleasantly round face and high cheekbones were flushed with the sheen of perspiration. Bobby was completely satisfied with himself, but after a few minutes of nuzzling against his chest she whispered, "Is everything okay, Bobby?"

"Why do you ask?" he said as nonchalantly as possible as inner alarm bells clanged.

"No reason... well, kind of. It's just that... you didn't seem quite yourself. Is anything the matter?"

*No, nothing, except the whole time I happened to be thinking of my wife.* "Maybe I have a little jet lag," he offered weakly.

"After a three-hour flight? You're silly," she said, playfully pinching his earlobe, another nuance of hers he'd forgotten over time. "It isn't *me*, is it?" she asked.

"Of course not," he said tenderly. "Jeez, Lulu, you're the most beautiful girl I've ever *seen*."

"Stop," she said teasingly. "You're making me blush."

"Okay, but I mean it," he repeated. And at that moment in 1979, he was being truthful.

"You're sweet," she said, and then coyly added, "You know, we've got a little time yet. Would you like to... you know... "

He couldn't decide what surprised him more—the fact that he immediately said yes, or that he'd actually be able to *do* it.

# Chapter Seven

"C'mon, you lovebirds, we've gotta get cracking," called Barnes as he rapped on the door. "Time's a-wasting and we have to get those bikes!"

Bobby opened the bungalow door and let his friend in. "Where's Tish?" he asked.

"Well, my man, since we decided to only get two double-seater bikes to save money, and since only you and I will be allowed to drive them, I figured what the hell, only the two of us have to go pick 'em up. Besides, for some reason I can't fathom, Tish is exhausted and needs a little nap." He gave a devilish wink.

"Ha ha, very funny," said Lucy, brushing her hair as she emerged from the bathroom. "Maybe I'll take a walk with her down to the beach; that is, if she's not too *exhausted*."

Bobby and Barnes sauntered over to the office and were soon being transported in the hotel taxi to the site of Oleander Cycles near Hamilton. "Can you actually believe we're here?" asked Barnes.

"It is pretty hard to believe," replied Bobby, the understatement of the year.

"Well, I don't mean to sound corny, but it's really cool being on a trip with you."

"Same here." And he truly meant it.

Bobby Romero and Barnes Nevin had been best friends since they had first met on the playground of their Catholic elementary school in the fifth grade and, naturally, gotten into a fight. After a truce was declared, they had joined forces and had been inseparable. Grades 5-8 at St. Mary's had been a hoot, with the dynamic duo getting in and out of scrapes and generally having a blast while trying to grow up in the restrictive atmosphere of Catholic school, where a whack over the head from the nuns was not uncommon, especially for Barnes.

The boys weren't exactly opposites, as they shared many of the same passions, among them a love of history, especially World War II, in which their fathers had proudly served; sports, most notably football; and of course, later on, pretty girls. Barnes was much more outgoing, the life of the party, while Bobby tended to be reserved in large groups, and more introspective. Thus, their personalities meshed perfectly, and they enjoyed playing off each other. "Like Butch Cassidy and the Sundance Kid," Barnes liked to say, citing their favorite teenage-era film. Barnes and Bobby would attend separate high schools (for some unfathomable reason Barnes would choose to continue his Catholic education from grades 9-12) where they would actually line up against each other (Barnes would always be a couple inches taller and ten pounds heavier), with Barnes as a hard-hitting strong safety and Bobby a shifty running back. Their dream of playing ball together would finally come true in college, as both contributed mightily to their team's success. Meanwhile, throughout their teen years they would double date, with Barnes's girlfriend frequency ratio around 2 to 1 as compared to Bobby's.

After college they'd drift apart for stretches but always find each other again. Bobby would be there for all three of Barnes's weddings (and breakups), as well as the death of his mother from lung cancer in the 1990s; similarly, Barnes would be included in the wedding party of Bobby and Valentina, and would become a virtual uncle to Michelle, even serving as her sponsor when she was confirmed in the Roman Catholic tradition. Sadly, none of Barnes's unions would produce a child, and Bobby always thought his buddy would have made a great father.

But of course, that all lay ahead for them, and Bobby was becoming more sure with every passing minute that he would be powerless to alert his friend as to what personal tragedies were down the road. He supposed that all he could do—as Barnes would do when Bobby's engagement would fall apart in less than a year—was to be there for him. But still, if there was a way to give him a heads-up, he had to try, if for no other reason than to save his mother, who was still smoking a pack a day in the late 70s. The question was, although the boys truly loved and trusted each other, would Barnes think Bobby was off his rocker if he *was* able to tell him he could see some forty years into his future?

* * *

After a cursory training course on the proper operation of a motor scooter and the signing of all necessary papers, the boys were taken out into the vast parking lot of Oleander Cycles and issued helmets for their test drive. True to their nature, Barnes was a little more daring in his maneuvers than the naturally cautious Bobby, but both clearly enjoyed riding the vehicles, made temporarily more powerful by the lack of someone in the passenger seat. They were also administered a somewhat stern lecture on the dangers of operating a motor scooter on Bermuda's winding, two-lane roads when impaired by drink or drugs, or banking too severely on a curve in the aftermath of the island's frequent pop-up showers, which tended to leave invisible oil slicks on the pavement. Bobby recalled the many accidents he'd witnessed over the years from tourists who were either drunk, too nervous, or showing off on their bikes. When he and Val had visited, they always rented a double seater, as operating a bike was too stressful for her. And after Michelle had come along, they'd stuck to taxis and Bermuda's famous pink buses for transportation.

The boys nodded seriously in response to their instructor's advice, took two more helmets for the girls, which were stowed in the bikes' front baskets, and headed back to the hotel, gradually increasing their speed as they became more comfortable. By the end of the drive, they were flying.

* * *

When the girls couldn't be found in the bungalows, Bobby and Barnes made their way out to the poolside bar where, sure enough, their ladies were enjoying a drink and dragging on cigarettes.

"Oh, oh," said Barnes. Although his pal couldn't have cared less, smoking was one of Bobby's pet peeves; both as a player and now a coach, he'd abhorred the habit. One of Bobby's high school girlfriends, Mandy, had smoked, and Bobby had never quite succeeded in convincing her to break what he considered an unhealthy, disgusting habit. His own dad had quit cold turkey in the late 60s, and his mom had never begun. Bobby failed to understand how people couldn't muster the willpower to overcome the urge. And, as a football coach and leader of young men, he'd be setting a poor example if his wife was seen in public puffing away. He'd never had such problems with Val, who was the epitome of decorum, so it was no wonder the old annoyance came back in a flash. "Easy, my man," cautioned Barnes.

Luckily, Lucy had seen him coming and, trying to avert a spat, quickly stubbed out her Winston. Tish didn't even flinch. But Bobby never had a chance to admonish Lucy, nor even shoot her a dirty look. He was waylaid by the tinny stereo speaker at the Tiki-style bar, from which wafted the familiar nasal voice of John Lennon singing "Imagine." For the second time that day, he felt horribly dizzy. *He's going to die*, thought Bobby. *Next year Mark David Chapman is going to shoot him outside his apartment building in New York City. Jesus Christ.*

As if reading his mind, Barnes asked the bar's patrons, "Hey, who thinks the Beatles might get back together?"

A couple with matching Hawaiian shirts raised their hands. "Don't I wish," said another guy with shoulder length hair before adding, "disco sucks."

"What about you, Bobby?" asked Lucy, sipping from her frozen Piña Colada. "If anybody wants to see them back together, it's you."

"Uh, I hope so," he replied, knowing full well it would never occur and trying not to betray the mix of sadness and impotency that had swept over him. He gritted his teeth; if saving Barnes's mom wasn't reason enough to try to alert others, maybe losing Lennon was.

"Sir? Excuse me, Sir? What will you be having?" asked the bartender as he placed a cardboard coaster before him.

"Oh, sorry, a Heineken," Bobby answered, hanging onto the polished teakwood bar for dear life as the world came back into focus.

"You kind of spaced out there," chided Lucy. "A penny for your thoughts?"

He smiled and said, "Nothing important." But he was thinking...

*The Disaster...*
John Lennon...
Barnes's mother...
*9/11.*

* * *

They spent the remainder of the afternoon down at the beach, the waves crashing with schools of fish roiling inside them. They were pleasantly surprised to find the sand was, indeed, pink, just like it said in the brochures their travel agent have provided. Tish sported a hot pink bikini, with Lucy tucked nicely into a red one-piece that made Bobby think of *Baywatch* back in the 90s. They slathered Coppertone or Hawaiian Tropic all over themselves (though Bobby knew full well he'd pay for it in the early 2000s, when he'd have to have a small piece of skin removed from his right temple near the hairline) and took turns venturing into the ocean to ride the waves and goof around. He and Lucy held hands and jumped the swells together, laughing and even hugging, and he ruefully thought, *Yeah, NOW she wants to hold on to me.*

As they later lay on their blankets, Bobby tried to formulate a game plan for how to conduct himself going forward, specifically how to approach Barnes, who was at the moment applying liberal doses of tanning oil to Tish's reddening shoulders. He spied Bobby looking over, winked mischievously, and said, "So, where to tonight, my man? What say we take the bikes into Hamilton for dinner?"

"Sounds great," he answered. And then he remembered: they would go to the Lobster Pot Restaurant that first night, and in the early morning hours Tish would have a reaction to the Coquille St. Jacques (scallops in cream sauce), rendering her useless until midmorning the next day. He smiled inwardly. Oh well. At least it hadn't been *his* idea.

Late that afternoon they climbed the long wooden staircase that hugged the cliffside, had another drink at the bar, and retired to their quarters to clean up and dress for the evening's activities. Bobby found himself inviting Lucy to join him in the shower, and she accepted—the first time he'd ever done this with a girl.

It was great.

* * *

Sometime near 7 PM they climbed aboard the double-seater scooters, put on their helmets, and took off for Hamilton, some twenty minutes away. Lucy held

Bobby tightly around the waist, the side of her helmet nestled against his broad shoulder, as he smoothly navigated the twists and turns of the South Road. Up ahead, his daredevil buddy cut the corners tightly, laughing with his girlfriend, who a couple times extended her arms like wings as they hit a straightaway.

They entered the quaint capital city by circling a roundabout, and then followed Front Street to the public scooter stand near the cruise ship dock. Horses and buggies were lined up at the curb, and Bobby recalled how he and Valentina had enjoyed a romantic ride on their honeymoon. He even remembered the name of the horse: Peanut. But he and his friends would skip the buggy ride on this trip, deeming it too expensive.

When Bobby asked for dinner suggestions, Barnes offered that the Lobster Pot looked cool in the Bermuda brochure. Thinking *You won't feel that way later on, buddy, when your girlfriend's Ralphing her guts out at the hotel,* he said, "Sounds great. I hope they actually have lobster on the menu."

"Or shrimp scampi," said Lucy, "although they probably don't make it the way I do." She wasn't much of a cook, Lucy Spencer, but her recipe for the dish, which she'd gotten from who knows where, called for the addition of tarragon to the traditional oil, garlic and white wine, and he loved it so much that he'd introduced it to Valentina (who was a *great* cook) early on. As it turned out, the recipe had outlasted Lucy by forty years, though every time they had it brought a moment or two of *agida* to Bobby.

Dinner at the Lobster Pot was fairly tasty and predictably expensive, especially when washed down with a bottle of white wine. Then they strolled down

Front Street, ducking in and out of classy department stores like Trimingham's and Brown & Company. When they passed Astwood Dickenson jewelers, Bobby was curious to see if his fiancée would pause to peruse the wedding bands on display in the window. She didn't.

Then it was on to Rum Runners, the local nightclub whose second deck porch overlooked Front Street, which was now bustling with tourists. They danced a little bit (not Bobby's strong suit) and had a couple cocktails before agreeing it had been an eventful first day and that a good night's sleep was in order if they wanted to get in some sightseeing the next morning. So, they paid their bar tab and made their way back to the bike stand, hopped on, and putt-putted back to the hotel, careful to observe the speed limit in the dark. The South Road was barely illuminated by the puny headlights of their vehicles, so it took a lot longer to get back. But Bobby didn't care. The smell of the salt air that washed over the cliffs made him want to take his time, Lucy was warm and soft pressed against his back, and the sight of the beacon from the Gibbs Hill lighthouse was really cool. He was almost sorry when they turned into the Reefside Apartments parking lot.

He was sorrier moments later when they passed the front desk. Lucy was a few steps ahead of him because he'd had to secure their helmets in the bike's basket. Apparently, Bobby's mother had called the hotel and left a message, asking if they'd made it there all right. But when the desk clerk tried to hail Lucy, calling out, "Mrs. Romero, ah, Mrs. Romero?" she just kept walking, like it didn't register at all.

*Hmmm.*

# Chapter Eight

The pink room phone on the night table next to Bobby gently rang at 8:30 the next morning. Groggily he reached out and picked up as Lucy pulled the covers over her head and burrowed more deeply into the mattress.

"Bad news, my man," said Barnes. "As it turns out, Tish is allergic to certain shellfish she ate last night and it was a barf-o-rama for a couple hours there."

"Jeez, sorry to hear that," said Bobby as sincerely as possible. "How is she now?"

"I wouldn't count on seeing her until midmorning at the earliest," he sighed. "Maybe I'll go for a run. Wanna come with me?"

"I don't know," he replied, "I mean, we're on vacation—"

"Yeah, but softball season starts when we get back, and I don't wanna be pulling muscles all over the place because I just sat on my ass for a week over here."

He had a point. Bobby and Barnes, along with a bunch of ex-footballers from school who had settled locally, had formed a beer league team called the Alums, who played in New Rochelle's very competitive "A" division of slow pitch softball. In fact, the team had been in operation even before they had graduated. Now the two of them were, in essence, the co-captains. Barnes was a power hitting leftfielder with an erratic cannon arm, while Bobby proved to be a more than adequate second baseman who usually led off in the lineup. He knew Barnes was right about getting their legs in shape, but was torn between running with his buddy and cuddling some more with Lucy. In the end, though, Barnes won, as Bobby determined that Lucy wouldn't be moving anywhere for at least a half-hour. "Okay, meet me outside in ten minutes," he said, and started rummaging in his suitcase for a tee shirt and shorts to wear.

He found his buddy sitting on a big rock outside the bungalow, tying his Adidas sneakers. "Good news, man," he said. "I was asking the girl behind the desk if there were any jogging paths nearby, and she said if we cross the South Road and go up one of those side streets they call tribal roads, we'll hit a trail that used to be the track bed for a small Bermuda railroad years ago. The tracks are gone but she said the scenery is really nice, like running in a tropical rain forest or some such shit."

"Sounds cool," said Bobby. "Let's do it."

They started at a slow jog across the two-lane South Road and labored up the tribal road for half a mile until they hit the historic Bermuda Railway Trail, bordered on both sides with lush greenery. A variety of birds sang in the canopy that partially blocked the morning sun. "Right or left?" asked Barnes, running in place.

"Left," said Bobby, remembering from his many walks with Val on that same path that they would eventually come out near the grounds of the famous Southampton Princess Hotel and Resort.

As the two best friends pounded along, Barnes suddenly said, "You know, sometimes Tish pisses me off."

"Really? How so?"

"Well, for one thing, do you know that she *knows* she's allergic to shellfish?"

"And she ate it anyway?"

"Yeah. It's like after a couple drinks, she just does stupid stuff."

"Huh," said Bobby, thinking, *Don't worry, man, you'll be dumping her inside of a year anyway.*

"I'll bet you don't have to worry about that with Lucy," he added.

"Why do you say that?"

"Because she's so, I don't know, *grounded*? Is that the word they use now? It just seems like you can always count on her to do the right thing." They ran a few more yards and he said, "I wish I had what you do, my man."

*No you don't,* thought Bobby.

\* \* \*

As predicted, Tish was indisposed this morning, so Bobby, Lucy and Barnes took breakfast at a South Road restaurant called the Parakeet and then stopped at the roadside market nearby to stock up on necessities for the week, most of which fell into the junk food/liquor categories. Of course, such staples as orange juice, milk, cereal (the breakfast menu at the Parakeet was ridiculously expensive) and coffee for the small machines in their rooms would at least allow them to begin their day; but six-packs of beer and bottles of wine filled a good part of the bikes' baskets, and Lucy was forced to use one hand to hold a plastic shopping bag filled with potato chips, pretzels and Doritos, along with crackers, blocks of cheese, and port wine-flavored Wispride spread. Their bill came to nearly $200, but they figured these "provisions" would at least last a few days.

Tish was there to meet them upon their return, sporting oversized sunglasses and a floppy straw hat to help combat her monstrous hangover. After a little good-natured ribbing (she even put down a few Ritz crackers, a good sign that she was recovering) they decided on visiting the Bermuda Aquarium in the Flatts section before pushing on to the Crystal Caves, another attraction.

On the ride to Flatts, Bobby couldn't shake the Lennon thing. All it took was one nutbag to put an official end to his childhood. The thing was, even as Bobby entered his 60s, the guy—Mike something or other—would still be in prison, and would probably never leave.

One thing Lucy sometimes got on him about was his somewhat narrow focus in music. But truthfully, he didn't see much worth listening to outside of the Beatles and his other favorites—the Beach Boys, the Stones, and Steely Dan. Steve Miller was okay, too, and Creedence. And he was always up for some good Motown like the Temptations or the Supremes. In the 80s he would enjoy the Police, Bob Seger, and Billy Joel as well, but that was after Lucy had left the scene. He couldn't stand disco, though, and thought it was a hoot when the Chicago White Sox had staged "Disco Demolition Night" at old Comiskey Park in July of '79, for which patrons of the doubleheader that day were urged to bring their disco records, which would be placed in a large box on the field between games and blown up. Although this would not happen for a few months, Bobby remembered the event as a fiasco, as the burgeoning crowd—far beyond the projected attendance for that evening—took the disco record detonation as a signal to storm the field. Things had gotten so out of hand, with many drunken fans tearing up the diamond, that the second game had to be forfeited. Disco itself would die a slow death over the next few years, while the classic rock that Bobby had always loved would live on.

But without John Lennon.

The Bermuda Aquarium was pleasant, with an eclectic mix of tropical fish and reptiles on display, as well as local flora, but Bobby was much more keen on seeing underwater life up close. He and his wife would do a lot of snorkeling on their subsequent trips, with Val eventually giving him a SCUBA course as a Christmas present in the early 2000s. But Lucy and Tish were fascinated by the creatures they saw today, so he played along with their enthusiasm, as did Barnes, who delighted in pointing out the ugliest features of each species, and two lizards that were apparently mating.

Then it was on to the Crystal Caves, some fifteen minutes farther east. Descending into the earth on a sloping wooden ramp, the foursome was greeted with blessedly cool air and a marvelous display of stalactites and the like that had them in awe—except for Barnes. When they emerged into the blinding sunlight some forty-five minutes later his first words were, "That was cool. Who wants to go grab a beer?"

They stopped at a roadside café just outside of Hamilton, had a burger and quenched their thirsts, and headed back to the hotel, where they agreed it was a pool kind of afternoon. As usual, the girls stood out among those who lounged in or near the water. After an hour or so, Bobby's thirst began to kick in, and he playfully asked Lucy, "So, Mrs. Romero, can I get you a cocktail?"

"That reminds me," she said. "There's something I want to talk to you about."

"Like what?"

"Well," she said cautiously, "I think that after we're married, I'd like to keep my name."

Bobby had never heard of such a thing, certainly not in his Italian family. "What do you mean?" he asked incredulously. "You don't... want to take my name?"

"No, no," she said coolly, "you're not getting what I mean. What I'm saying is, I want to hyphenate my name. You know, Spencer-Romero. Isn't that okay?"

He looked at her, and a little voice in his head said, *Hey man, by the 90s everybody was doing this. Think of all the kids you would be teaching whose moms' and dads' names were different, even if they weren't divorced or separated. She's just ahead of the curve here.* But he said, "I don't get it. I think it's ridiculous."

He waited for her to back down, but she didn't. "Well, I think I want to do it," she said firmly.

"Can we talk about it later?" he said, obviously pissed off. "I'm going to the bar to get a drink. You want one?"

"No, thank you," she said frostily.

He shrugged his shoulders. "Suit yourself, Lulu." He started forward, then found himself turning back. "And don't worry," he added sarcastically, "I won't call you 'Mrs. Romero' anymore." He knew he'd hurt her, but hey, she'd insulted him first, right? It wasn't until he'd taken his first sip of beer at the bar that he realized what an asshole he'd been. But he wouldn't— *couldn't*—apologize.

\* \* \*

By the time they'd returned to the bungalow and showered—separately—it was getting close to dinner. "Want some cheese and crackers and a glass of wine before we go out?" he asked her, toweling off his hair before attacking it with the blow dryer.

"That would be nice, thanks," she replied, and he sensed a slight thaw. Lucy had already slipped into a yellow sundress and looked smashing.

"That's a great dress, Lulu," he said.

"You think so? I just got it last week."

"It looks like it was made for you."

"Thanks," she said, and kissed him on the cheek; a positive sign, he hoped.

\* \* \*

Dinner that night was that King Henry VIII, just a short drive farther on down the South Road. The place was a little over the top, very medieval, with "wenches" in 1600s period garb serving up such English favorites as shepherd's pie and bangers and mash. The couples got right into it, ordering pints of ale before the meal, with

Barnes even affecting a Tudoresque brogue when addressing their good-natured waitress, who, like the others, was attired in a low-cut peasant dress that accentuated her cleavage. Of course, the women at Bobby's table were no slouches either in that department, but Barnes delighted in playfully tormenting the fresh-faced Bermudian lass.

They were just tucking into their dinners when Tish noted that everyone in their party was either of British or Irish descent—except Bobby, who was equal parts Sicilian and Southern Italian. And although the conversation was light hearted and playful, Bobby's grandmother's words came back to him as he chewed his steak and kidney pie. He watched Lucy from the corner of his eye as she chatted away between sips of beer, recalling the name- taking thing earlier in the day, and he thought, *Who are you?*

But there was something else nagging him. He didn't know why, but he kept looking around for Valentina, like she was just going to pop up and say, "Dream's over, honey. Time to get up, we've got an 8 AM tee time."

Even Barnes noticed. "You need something?" he asked.

"Uh, I'm out of water," he said, recovering nicely.

"Allow me. Wench! Water, please!" he bellowed.

"You're such a nut," said Tish, draining her second pint.

Bobby smiled weakly, then stole a glance at Lucy. She'd noticed, too.

By the time they motored back to the hotel, pleasantly buzzed and filled with their British meat and potatoes, Bobby had shaken the negativity that had come over him during dinner, and that night's lovemaking betrayed no ill feelings from earlier in the day. But instead of looking forward to the next day's planned trip to the quaint St. George's on the eastern tip of the island, Bobby felt like he was coaching a football game where his team was behind and the clock was ticking down. He only had a few days left to solve the mystery of Lucy Spencer.

# Chapter Nine

The headaches started the next morning as he lay staring at the rotating wooden blades of the overhead fan. Bobby noticed that whenever he began concentrating on the future—especially anything having to do with Valentina—little spots would start exploding behind his eyeballs. It was disconcerting, especially when he was in the throes of passion and saw her face, or when he was driving the motorbike and remembered places they'd visited. He quietly got up, padded over to his travel kit in the bathroom, and took a couple aspirin with a glass of tap water. It tasted a little funny, and he wished bottled water had been popular back in '79. If so, they would've picked up a case. Maybe that was the problem; he had been drinking a disproportionate amount of alcohol to water on this trip. Perhaps he was just dehydrated? Bobby put down two more glasses of Bermuda tap water and returned to bed.

He'd barely laid back down when Lucy turned over and faced him, her blonde hair obscuring most of her soft features, her lips parted slightly as she slept. He realized that neither of them had yet to pass gas in bed, and though it pained him to think of it, he remembered how Val would punch him in the arm every time he let one go, even if he offered an "excuse me." Of course, over the 30+ years of marriage, they'd been through a lot worse, including the times he had to hold her up over the toilet with morning sickness when Michelle had come along. And, later, when he'd had his hip replacement, the times she had to hold *him* up during the night those first couple weeks as he peed into a plastic bottle so he wouldn't have to make the journey to the bathroom. He wondered if he and Lucy would've had so intimate a relationship.

Just then her eyes opened. "Why are you staring at me?" she murmured.

"'Cause you're pretty. Go back to sleep."

"'Kay." She rolled back over.

\* \* \*

The ride to St. George's, the original capital of Bermuda, was a long one, with the couples having to pass through five "parishes" to reach the island's eastern end. But once there, they were entranced with its quaint charm, from the names of side streets like Featherbed Alley and Petticoat Lane, to the old wooden prisoner stocks and ducking stool near the Village Square dock. They meandered through various small shops, hand-in-hand, with Bobby trying mightily to avoid looking for Val. Like most tourists, they took photos of each other in the 2-person stocks—with their Kodak Instamatic cameras, of course—and then had a bite to eat at a café overlooking the Square. Bobby had taken a liking to Bermuda fish chowder, laced with dark rum and hot sherry peppers, which he'd first tasted as an appetizer at the Lobster Pot. With a cold pint and a piece of crusty bread, he was in heaven, despite the heat of the day that usually precluded the ingesting of hot soup. Just to be safe, though, he also drank a few glasses of water.

From there the couples visited nearby Fort St. Catherine, where both Barnes and Bobby enjoyed the nautical museum and large iron cannons that protruded from the fort's 18th-century battlements that had guarded Bermuda from pirate attack. After a little clowning around from the boys, which included a mock sword fight on the outer wall of the fort, they decided that since it was late afternoon already, and the ride home would be very long, that they simply stop midway in Hamilton for dinner before spending the evening at Astwood Beach Park near the hotel.

"Well, we did the British thing last night," said Barnes, removing his helmet at the Hamilton motorbike stand, "so how about some Italian, in honor of Bobby?"

"Great idea," said Tish, who would've eaten anything, as long as drinks came with it.

They came upon La Trattoria, on a side street off Front, where they shared a mediocre Bermudian pizza and some appetizers, along with a bottle of Chianti. Then they walked it off a little before mounting their bikes for the trip home.

It had been a long day, but even so, the young couples weren't tired yet, so they ventured over to the cliffs of Astwood Park that overlooked the Atlantic. Barnes gave Bobby a wink, their signal from way back that it was time to split up, and minutes later he found himself and Lucy perched on a flat rock looking out over the vast ocean. The sun had set, but there was still enough light to see, and the salt air had yet to cool. He remembered, with a stab of pain, how he and Val had done pretty much the same thing on the first night of their honeymoon in '86. She had said, simply, "I can't believe we're finally married. I'm so happy." The memory made him sad and wistful.

"Bobby, did you hear me?" asked Lucy.

"What?"

"Did you hear what I said?"

"Uh, no, sorry, Lulu. I was spacing out. What did you say?"

"I asked you if you were happy."

"Of course I am. Why do you ask?"

"I don't know," she said, resting her head on his shoulder. "Lately, at times you've been, uh, a little distracted."

He was right. Shit, she definitely had noticed. "Like how?"

"I don't know how to put it," she said carefully. "It's like, you're checking around, like you're afraid someone's watching you."

"Jeez, sorry," he said. "I'm just, like, taking everything in, I guess," he tried. "And of course, I'm making sure nobody's checking you out."

"Sure you are," she said with a chuckle.

"Lucy," he began, wanting so much to try to somehow get her to divulge some deep, dark secret that would hold the key to his impending misery.

"Yes?" She looked him full in the face, the ocean breeze riffling her hair.

"I… " He tried mightily to get the words out but the explosions in his head began again, worse than the morning. He took a deep breath. "We, uh, should head back before it's too dark to see on these rocks."

"Good idea," she said.

He stood, shakily, put his arm around his fiancée, and walked her back to the bungalow.

* * *

"Want me to freshen up a bit?" asked Lucy as he began undressing.

"Sure thing," he replied, and within seconds he could hear the shower running. The wind was now coming in off the water, and carried with it the sounds of revelers at the Tiki bar as they enjoyed a nightcap. The radio was playing that ridiculous song "Midnight at the Oasis," and the thought came to Bobby about how horrible the current top 40 songs were, and how he longed for the Beatles. But then, he paused.

John Lennon... John Lennon. Something about John Lennon. What was it?

He'd forgotten.

At that moment Lucy emerged from the bathroom, a towel wrapped around her. The lights were out, and her young body was silhouetted against the bungalow's thinly veiled bedroom window. Then she let the towel drop, and Bobby's breath caught in his throat.

Ah, well. Whatever it was about John Lennon, it couldn't have been that important.

* * *

The next morning Bobby was again coerced into joining Barnes for a morning run, and they followed the same route. "Man, my legs are done after last night," bragged his buddy. "Tish was really into it."

"Uh-huh," said Bobby, who had never been one to kiss and tell, despite pressure from his sometimes overbearing teammates.

"You guys have a fun night?"

"Yup."

"Well, okay then," laughed Barnes, knowing it was pointless to press him on it. "Hey, Bobby, let's say you and Lucy get married—"

"Of course we're gonna get married," snapped Bobby. "Or hadn't you heard that we're engaged?"

"No, I mean... let me start again. Okay, let's say you're married, and you go on your honeymoon, and all that. And then it's time to settle down, have kids and all. Do you think it'll ever, uh, *get old* with you and Lucy?"

"Not a chance," he said all-too-truthfully. "But why are you asking me this?"

"I dunno," he huffed as they sped along. "With Tish and me, it's like, I find it hard to imagine us in like, ten years. And even though she's ungodly sexy, I worry sometimes that I won't be able to, you know, stay loyal to one woman."

Oh, how Bobby longed to clue his friend in to the fact that he was to average about 5 ½ years per marriage down the road, with lots of women in between. But as far as he knew, infidelity on his friend's part would never be the cause of any of the bust-ups.

He could see that his dear friend was in need of reassurance, words of wisdom—or warning—*something*, but as he opened his mouth to speak his sneaker caught in a leaf-covered tree root and he went down like he'd been shot.

Barnes pulled up. "Hey, you okay?" he asked as Bobby embarrassedly got to a knee and wiped dirt off his backside.

"Yeah," he answered. "No big deal. But, Barnes?"

"Yeah?"

"Listen, you're the most loyal guy I know," he managed. "So I wouldn't worry about it."

Barnes brightened. "I was hoping you'd say that," he said, extending his hand to help Bobby up. "Want to keep going?"

"Let's turn back," said Bobby. "I think I'm getting thirsty."

"That's what I'm *talkin'* about!" crowed his friend, and they slapped a high-five.

\* \* \*

Jobson's Cove is a picturesque little nook in the expanse of Astwood Beach, with huge, arching boulders framing a small patch of sand and allowing inside only a translucent pool of seawater no deeper than waist high. It was usually mobbed, especially with little kids, but today the foursome had it all to themselves. They spread a couple blankets and waded into the cooling water. The day was unseasonably warm for April, and the usually constant ocean breeze had evaporated, so the water offered instant relief, and they floated around on their stomachs, trying to catch a glimpse of the small tropical fish that darted in and out of the cove.

Once back on the blankets, it was time to grease up and sunbathe (Tish rolled down her top until it barely covered her nipples) and enjoy some iced-down beers that Barnes had thrown in a small Styrofoam cooler he'd found in his bungalow's kitchen. A bag of Doritos completed the mid-day snack.

A while later, Barnes, ever the restless one, announced he was going for a walk down the beach in search of seashells to bring home to his mom. When no one else expressed the desire to move from their spot, he shrugged and took off alone. Within minutes he had vanished in the distance.

It was at this moment that Tish went into action. She always enjoyed tweaking Bobby, whom she considered too conservative for his age, and with Barnes gone the opportunity presented itself. Before either he or Lucy could react, she'd produced a joint and started puffing away. "Tish, where did you get *that*?" Bobby spluttered.

"Sneaked it in," she replied proudly, and took a hit.

Lucy remained silent.

"But… what if customs had caught you?"

"I only brought in a teeny bit," she giggled. "And where I had it hidden, they didn't *dare* look."

Bobby fought hard not to take the bait, and managed a weak "Oh."

But Tish kept pressing. "Hey, Lucy, you know what? I've been really wanting to try out those scooters for myself. I mean, why should the guys have all the fun? What do you say we go for a ride?"

Bobby was sure that Lucy would quash such an outlandish suggestion, but instead she appeared to be seriously considering the offer. Finally he said, in measured tones, "Listen, Tish, those bikes are signed out to me and Barnes, and I doubt if you're insured to drive them—"

"Ah, Barnes won't mind," she replied airily, waving the joint in his face. "Don't be such a wet blanket, *Coach*. Hey Lucy, you comin' with me or not?"

Bobby turned to his fiancée with an expression reflecting a combination of hope and desperation, but all he got in return was a cold, impassive look, one that would be repeated months later in a Mexican restaurant. "Where are the keys, Bobby?" she said as matter-of-factly as if she was asking for the time of day.

"On the kitchenette table," he replied stonily, his heart sinking.

Tish, flashing a triumphant smile, stood and brushed the sand from her bikini bottom. "Ta-ta," she said, and made for the staircase. With hardly a glance back, Lucy followed. They climbed the cliffside, Tish at one point missing a step and almost falling back into Lucy, who giggled. Bobby sat impotently, watching their laborious ascent, until they cleared the top of the bluff and were gone.

"Hey, where are the girls?" said Barnes, materializing a few minutes later with a handful of shells jangling between his fingers.

"They went for a scooter ride," said Bobby.

"*What?*" But they never learned how to work the bikes!"

"I'm aware of that," said Bobby resignedly.

"But what if they crash them?"

"Then I guess we have a problem."

Barnes was incredulous. "Jesus Christ, Bobby, why didn't you stop them?"

"Well, Barnes, because your girlfriend, who by the way was toking on a joint she'd smuggled onto the island, decided she was going to break my stones and drag Lucy along."

"And Lucy was *okay* with this?"

"Apparently."

"Jeez, I would've never thought—"

"Me neither."

Barnes fell silent, with only the lapping of the waves between them. After a few awkward seconds Bobby said, "I'm gonna go for a walk."

"Want some company?"

"Nah, that's okay," he said. "Gotta clear my head." Wisely, his best buddy let him go.

* * *

When he returned a half-hour later, Bobby was surprised to find the girls laid out on the blankets, with Tish fast asleep next to Barnes, who was reading a *Sports Illustrated*.

"Hi," said Lucy as he sat down next to her.

"Hi."

"Want to go for a dip with me?"

"Sure."

They waded out into the tidal pool, until they were at its farthest point from the beach. Then Lucy sat down on a submerged boulder, the water almost reaching her throat. Bobby did the same. "So, how was your bike ride?" he asked as nonchalantly as possible.

"We didn't end up going."

"How come?"

"Tish couldn't find where Barnes had left the keys."

"Oh. But if she had?"

"Then we would've done it."

"I see."

She turned to him, the sun glinting off her hair. "Listen," she said quietly. "I know you care, and I know it hurts your pride or whatever when I don't act the way you want me to, but you have to understand that I don't like being dictated to."

Bobby managed a "But—" before Lucy raised her hand, which broke the water, to silence him.

"Let me finish," she said. "You have very set ideas about how things work, and for the most part we agree on them. But I will *not* have you think for me, not now or ever. And don't *ever* try to tell me what to do, Bobby. I'm my own person, and you'd better realize that." She paused and then added, "You've still got a lot to learn about me."

"Okay, Lulu," he said, thinking *So that was when it all started.*

And he ached for his wife.

# Chapter Ten

That night was to be a special occasion: the weekly seafood buffet on the expansive patio of the Elbow Beach Resort a mile or so down the South Road. Since it was said to be a fairly upscale affair, the girls chose sundresses and the guys golf shirts and khakis.

Barnes and Tish came by Bobby's bungalow before they left for a pre-dinner glass of wine, and all seemed to be well. Tish even sidled up to Bobby while he was pouring potato chips into a bowl and gave his arm a rub. "Sorry, Coach," she said without sarcasm, "I wasn't thinking on the beach today. Don't be mad with Lucy."

"No problem," he whispered back.

Overall, the evening promised to be a good one. There was a slight breeze coming off the water, and the moon was full, without a cloud in the sky. The couples were shown to their table, and as usual, the girls turned some heads.

They were waiting to place their drink order when Tish asked, "So, how does the softball team look for this year? Are you guys going to do any better?"

"Well, second place last year wasn't too bad," corrected Barnes, "but we missed the playoffs. I think we'll take our division this year. It's just a question of how well we'll hit in the clutch. We left so many guys on base last season it was ridiculous. I mean, most of the time Bobby led off the game with either a hit or a walk, and he got stranded too many times."

"Our defense could be a little better, too," chipped in Bobby. "Sometimes we just look like a bunch of football players trying to play softball."

"Well, that's what you *are*," said Lucy brightly, and they all laughed.

"I just hope we get off to a better start than the Yankees have," said Barnes. "I mean, I know they won the World Series the past two years, but if they don't get it together soon that asshole Steinbrenner will fire Bob Lemon and bring back Billy Martin ahead of time."

Bobby nodded. The Yankees' mercurial manager had been dismissed midseason the year before with his team some fourteen games behind the hated Boston Red Sox after suffering what seemed to be some kind of nervous breakdown, reportedly fueled by a bad drinking habit. Lemon, a Hall of Fame pitcher in his day, had been brought in as a change of pace and the team, nicknamed "The Bronx Zoo," seemed to respond to his laid-back style, eventually tying the Sox for the division lead on the last day of the regular season before defeating them in a dramatic one-game playoff in Fenway Park and capturing the American League pennant and the World Series.

However, in a dramatic move during the Yankees' annual Old-Timers Day commemoration just scant days after Martin's tearful termination, it was announced that he would return for the 1980 season, which left Lemon in a precarious position. The Yankees needed to get off to a fast start in '79 for Lemon to keep his job for the entire season, but his status was tenuous at best.

"I think a lot of it depends on Reggie Jackson, and if he and Thurman Munson can get along," observed Barnes. Even during the best of times, the relationship between the brash slugger and the Yankee catcher was shaky, and the addition of the temperamental Martin and the meddlesome Steinbrenner only fueled the fire.

"Yeah," said Bobby, "Jackson's the superstar, but Munson's the captain, and the guys listen to him." No sooner had the words left his mouth then he got a searing pain behind his eyes. What was *this* about? He wasn't thinking about Val... did it have something to do with Thurman Munson? As much is it pained him, he dug deep into his future memory, then looked up as a low-flying airliner droned overhead on its descent toward the airport.

But then, as quickly as the pain had hit him, it was gone.

"And what will you be having to drink with your meal tonight, ladies and gentlemen?" asked the dark-skinned waiter, clad in a white jacket and shirt with black tie and trousers. The girls ordered Swizzles while Barnes and Bobby went the beer route. They were then free to avail themselves to the sumptuous buffet laid out on long, white linen-covered tables.

"Man, I don't know where to start," said Barnes, perusing the seemingly endless chafing dishes.

"King crab legs for me," said Bobby happily, and he plucked a few to start his food pile. He added a couple lobster tails and shrimp before ending with sea scallops.

Tish, to her credit, had learned her lesson, and stuck to filet of sole, avoiding all types of shellfish. She even selected a chicken breast, provided for those with the same dietary restrictions as her.

They returned to the table, the boys' plates groaning with food. Lucy, who'd helped herself to a modest portion of scallops in cheese sauce over rice, said, "You *are* allowed to get seconds, guys."

Just then the evening's entertainment, in the form of the island's premier Caribbean band, the Bermuda Strollers, launched into a somewhat up-tempo version of "Yellow Bird" while introducing themselves and inviting everyone to dance. It made for a pleasant tableau: the linen tables and waiters' attire contrasted nicely with the colorful tropical shirts and dresses of the patrons. The moon beamed on the beach and the breakers frothed on the shoreline, while the soothing tones of steel drums mingled with the calling of seagulls and longtails overhead. If Bobby could have ordered up a romantic setting for his reconciliation with Lucy, this would be it.

So, when Barnes, who had polished off his first plate of food, grabbed Tish's hand and led her onto the dance floor, Bobby turned to his fiancée. "Want to dance, Lulu?" he asked hopefully.

"Sure," she said, and he inwardly sighed with relief.

Bobby normally avoided dancing, primarily because he was bad at it, but Lucy was pretty smooth. She let him lead, if one could call it that; actually, they just kind of shuffled around to the slow tune the Strollers were playing, "Bermuda is Another World." Lucy, a couple inches shorter than Bobby even in heels, lay her head on his shoulder and looped her hands around his neck, while he encircled her trim waist and pulled her close. He took in the fragrance of her Herbal Essence shampoo and that infernal L'air du Temps and wondered how on earth it could all possibly go so wrong mere months from now.

"Having fun, Lulu?" he asked.

"You know it," she whispered in his ear.

He was so overcome with emotion that he couldn't help saying it: "I love you, Lucy."

She looked up into his face, the moonlight reflecting in her eyes, and kissed him. "I know," she said quietly.

* * *

After some more food, dancing, and a few more drinks, the conversation flowed freely among the friends, who had managed to save a little room for the dessert table selection. "Christ, only three days more for you guys, and two for us," said Barnes as he popped a mini éclair into his mouth. "This vacation is flying by."

"Well, we've done a lot, and seen a lot so far," said Bobby. "How about tomorrow? I'm told the Royal Dockyard is pretty cool."

"Where's that?" asked Tish, sipping another cocktail.

"All the way on the West End," he answered. "I'd estimate it's around a half hour drive with the scooters from the hotel."

"What's there to see?" asked Barnes.

"More museum-type stuff, but there's also a couple bars—"

"I'm in!" cried Tish.

"Okay then, it's decided," said Bobby. "But I am *not* running tomorrow morning. Let's sleep in a little while, okay?"

"That sounds great," agreed Lucy. They finished their coffees and strolled down to the beach, hand-in-hand. Once there they removed their shoes and the boys rolled up their pant legs so they could walk in the surf. The water was cool in the sand soft between their toes. Soon, Barnes and his girlfriend were standing calf-deep in the water, kissing passionately as the undertow sloshed against their bare legs.

"Romantic," said Bobby, and Lucy chuckled. "But Barnes is right—this week is flying by. It's gonna be over before we know it."

"So let's make it last," she said, and kissed him tenderly.

And as he held her that night under the stars, Bobby thought, *I wish I could freeze this moment forever*, but the knowledge that it would never be recaptured broke his heart.

\* \* \*

Unable to fall asleep that night, Bobby lay there weighing his options as to how to deal with the current situation. Option one was to go ahead and try to alter the path he was on by sharing his knowledge of the future with Barnes and trying to prevent what would happen. But he was quickly reminded of one of his favorite stories that he taught at school, "The Monkey's Paw," by W.W. Jacobs, in which an old man acquires a magical talisman that will allow him three wishes, but which comes with a warning: that any man who tries to change his fate does so at his own risk. Sure enough, the man gains the wealth he wishes for with the paw, but loses his beloved son in the process.

This story always led to some lively class discussion with his students, and the question as to whether any of them would risk changing their fate. And, of course, the kids would always turn the question on him: "Coach Romero, if you could change your future, would you? Even if it could lead to something really bad?" And he would always answer, "Well, I would have to know that what was up ahead was terrible. Then, I'd have to make my decision." But he'd never told his students he would actually *do* it. So, the dilemma remained: if Bobby tried to alter the future, would it start a chain reaction that could make his world even worse?

Option two was (if this was indeed more than a dream and some kind of "Groundhog Day" deal) that he simply ride it out for the next few years, have his life destroyed, while hanging onto the hope that he would meet Valentina, and that it would all work out in the end.

Option three was kind of a compromise. Perhaps he could enlist Barnes to assist him in his quest for the truth without trying to actively change his fate. Of course, Barnes's M.O. was to help out any friend in need, so that wasn't a problem; but would this alternate plan be enough to spare Bobby the possible penalty?

And then, there was one more thing that he had recently begun to consider, and it chilled him: What if this really *was* 1979, and the whole narrative in his head about Valentina Dominguez and the future was a figment of his imagination? What if he was actually suffering from some kind of psychosis and he was, in effect, cracking up? Could it be possible that a crazy person have such clear "memories" of future events? It frightened him to think about it.

As he turned over these thoughts, Lucy suddenly rolled toward him and unconsciously flung an arm across his chest before resuming her blissful slumber. *Please*, he thought, *if this is a dream, let me wake up. I want to go back, if there's somewhere to go back to.* He finally fell into a restless sleep, accompanied by a sense of foreboding that something was about to happen.

* * *

It was about 3 o'clock the next morning when Bobby sat bolt upright in bed, wide awake, his mind a whirling jumble.

Eleven... Beatles... Munson... Lennon... Nine... Michelle... Val...

Barnes.

He staggered to the bathroom, shut the door and barely made it to the toilet before puking up the prodigious amount of food and drink he'd put down hours before. His head was spinning and he hugged the bowl for dear life. *You're losing it,* his addled mind told him, *your future memories are fading, and fast. You've gotta do something before it's too late.* He literally crawled out of the bathroom to the bedroom, where Lucy softly snored under the covers. Blindly, he fumbled through the top drawer of his nightstand where he'd earlier spied some hotel stationery and a pen. He retreated to the bathroom, lay on the cool tile floor, and started to scribble furiously. He'd never done something so hard; it was like all the tortuous double session summer football practices he'd endured in high school and college rolled into one. Every word brought more stabbing head pain, weakness and nausea, but he pushed through somehow, summoning all the mental toughness he had. By the time he finished and sealed the paper in a hotel envelope, he was more tired than he'd ever been in his life, but also strangely relieved.

Bobby slipped the envelope into his suitcase, climbed into bed next to his sleeping fiancée, and was out cold in seconds.

* * *

When he awoke the next morning, around 8 AM, he felt no ill effects of the previous night, save for a little dry mouth. He knew he'd been deathly sick, but attributed it to a toxic mix of seafood buffet and alcohol. He also suspected there was something more to the ordeal, but couldn't put his finger on it.

It was while he was pondering all this that Lucy entered in a clingy tank top and cutoffs, holding a steaming cup of coffee. "Well, it's about time, sleepyhead," she said playfully. "I tried to wake you up like an hour ago, but you wouldn't budge. Were you okay last night?"

"I think I overdid it," he said, the understatement of the year. "The thing is, I'm hungry as hell."

"Well, if you want to eat something before we leave for the Dockyard, you'd better get moving."

"Got it." Bobby rolled out of bed and found that he felt refreshed, even energized. After quickly showering he wolfed down some orange juice, coffee, and cereal. He remembered what had happened the day before at the beach, but also that things had been worked out, and that the evening at Elbow Beach had been magical.

But that was *all* he remembered.

# Chapter Eleven

The Royal Naval Dockyard on Bermuda's western tip had been the principal base of the British Navy for the centuries spanning the American Revolution to the Cold War. At first it housed defenses to ward off attacks from France, but it was later used as a stopoff or supply depot for the Royal Navy during various wars. By the time of Bobby's 1979 visit, the site had fallen somewhat into disrepair, although multiple cannons, anchors and other vestiges of Britain's storied naval heritage dotted the walled battlements.

The trip to the West End was a long yet scenic one. Following the South Road, they left Warwick Parish and crossed into Southampton Parish, where the island began to bend northward. The Gibbs Hill lighthouse, King Henry VIII Restaurant, and St. Agnes Church, its whitewashed above-ground burial crypts baking in the blinding late morning sun, and various beaches, such as church Bay, Turtle Bay, and Whale Bay, offering scenic overlooks, saw them pass. They went by old Fort Scour and then entered Sandy's Parish, gliding through quaint hamlets where the welcoming residents invariably waived a hello. The couples even stopped for a photo at Somerset Bridge, regarded as the world's smallest drawbridge, which had stood on the same site since 1620. Finally, they crossed a short causeway to the Royal Navy Dockyard, whose protective walls towered above the shoreline, and pulled over to park.

"Whew," said Barnes, slipping off his helmet and shaking out his Bruce Jenner-like coif. "I was getting hot in there." Luckily, there was a roadside stand nearby where they purchased an iced tea to tide them over.

The museum there wasn't much to speak of; it seemed that it had been kind of thrown together. The displays were a bit careworn, and barely held the attention of the group. However, the gift shop did provide an interesting moment for Bobby. At one point, Lucy was rummaging around in a bin of rather garish sunglasses and pulled out a pair to try on. Once she had them set she placed a hand behind her head, mussed hair a bit, threw out a hip and pursed her lips. "What do you think, Bobby?" she asked.

He just smiled and said, "Perfect," wishing that he could bed her right there and then. Unfortunately, they were a long way from the hotel, and he was almost sorry he'd recommended the trip, for the entire Dockyard complex appeared a little run down.

"They should fix this place up," said Barnes. "It could really be cool. Some shops and restaurants like in St. George's would help. I bet cruise ships would even dock here."

"Speaking of restaurants," said Tish, "it's after noon and I'm starving. Bobby, you said we could get something to eat and drink here?"

"Yeah, according to a brochure I read. Let's explore a bit." Sure enough, they found a hole-in-the-wall café that catered mostly to the locals and shared some delicious fried fish sandwiches, washed down with ice cold beers.

"I say we go back and get in the water," suggested Barnes. "What do you guys think—beach or pool?" It ended up 3-1 in favor of the beach (Tish wanted to get a drink at the pool bar), and they climbed aboard the scooters for the ride back.

It was at the beach, while standing thigh-deep in the crashing waves of Astwood Park, that Barnes had one of his "moments of enlightenment" as Bobby called them. "Guess what, ladies?" he announced. "You're in for a treat tonight. Bobby and I are going to cook you dinner!"

This was news to Bobby. "With what? Doritos and potato chips? Or maybe a Wispride cheese soufflé?"

"Nah, you and I will take a ride to the market down the road and pick up the supplies. We'll figure out what we're having when we see what they've got."

Bobby shook his head, thinking, *typical Barnes.* But the girls readily agreed to the plan, so he had no choice.

They stayed at the beach until late afternoon, Barnes and Tish enjoying their last day on the pink sand, and then the guys dropped the girls off at the poolside bar before heading to the market. Once there, it was difficult to find food that was easy to cook without purchasing additional condiments, or that wasn't terribly expensive.

"Well, there are no grills at the hotel, so steaks and burgers and such are out," said Bobby. "Want to bake a chicken?" He had become a fairly good cook over the years, both by watching his mother and through trial and error during summer football practice, when the rest of the family was away at the shore and he (usually with the help of Barnes) had to raid the freezer and fend for himself.

"Chicken's good, but with what?" asked Barnes. "We need something on the side."

"Well, we've got milk and butter at the hotel," reasoned Bobby, "so let's get a chicken, a box of Stovetop stuffing, instant mashed potatoes, some chicken gravy and canned peas. That should do it. Like a mini-Thanksgiving in Bermuda."

"The ladies will be impressed, and all too happy to show their gratitude, surely."

"One would think," said Bobby with a smile.

"And for dessert?"

"I saw some Sara Lee cakes in the fridge," he said, hooking a thumb over his shoulder. "Go pick one."

"Got it."

After adding a six-pack and a bottle of white wine, they were ready to load their cycle baskets. The tab wasn't cheap, but still much less than a night out in Hamilton. Besides, everyone seemed to want to just kick back and enjoy their last night together. It was decided that Bobby and Lucy would host, because Barnes and Tish had to pack for their early-morning flight out the next day. By the time Bobby returned to the bungalow, Lucy had already showered and was stretched out on the couch, reading a paperback she'd found on the shelf. "Need help?" she asked.

"No, you relax," he said. "Let's just hope this oven works." He melted some butter and rubbed it over the chicken, then added some salt and pepper. Luckily, there was a baking dish in the small cupboard, and he shoehorned the chicken into it before setting the electric oven. Once that was done, he took a shower, whistling a Beatles tune as he looked forward to a (hopefully) delicious meal.

After a prolonged cocktail hour during which the foursome cleaned out the remainder of their snack food, Bobby and Barnes prepared the stuffing, mashed potatoes, gravy and peas, alternating the two small saucepans in the bungalow. Finally they served it up, the girls applauding their efforts. "This chicken is great, Bobby," said Tish. "Really tender."

"Glad you like it," he said, swigging his beer. The atmosphere was warm and friendly, and he was sorry the week was coming to an end.

As if reading his mind, Barnes tapped his beer bottle with a fork. "I propose a toast: to a great week with good friends in a beautiful place."

"Hear, hear!" blurted Tish, who was well into her cups.

Barnes shook his head and continued. "As I was saying, I hope someday we can all come back here together and do it again. And while I'm on it, I'd like to toast our hosts, Bobby and Lucy, who invited us on this trip. All I can say is that we're both so happy for you, and wish you all the best of luck. I can't think of a better couple to have as friends."

"Thanks, man," said Bobby.

Lucy just smiled and raised her glass of chablis in salute.

By the time dessert was over, everyone was full and a little buzzed, except for Tish, who was fairly plastered. "Ladies, if you don't mind," said Bobby, "I'd like to take a last bike ride with my buddy here."

"Sure, you two go," said Lucy. "I'll straighten up."

"And I'll go back to our room," said Tish. "I need an Alka-Seltzer."

"Just give me a second," said Bobby. He went into the bedroom to his suitcase, where he had a surprise for his best buddy that he'd been saving. It had become a tradition for the guys to enjoy a "victory stogie" after wins on the college football field. Neither was a cigarette smoker, and neither inhaled the sometimes noxious cigars they selected, but it was a male bonding kind of thing. The girls thought it was gross, and Lucy usually wouldn't go anywhere near Bobby after he'd had one until he'd used mouthwash and brushed his teeth. Still, they had a bit of fun with it, acting like big shots and blowing smoke rings.

But when he opened his suitcase he saw something else on top—an envelope upon which he'd inscribed "Give to Barnes—open back home." Vaguely, he remembered writing it the previous night, but had forgotten its contents. And he'd sealed it. *Ah, well,* he thought to himself, *it's probably something corny about what a great friend he is and all that. It's always been easier for me to say things on paper, anyway.* So, he stuffed the envelope in his jeans pocket, found the cigars, and closed the suitcase.

"Ready to roll?" asked Barnes as he emerged from the bedroom. "You were in there a long time."

"Sorry. Let's get going."

The night air actually had a chill to it; they'd been predicting a cold front to blow in near the end of the week, and this suggested its beginning. The boys went back to their rooms for a light jacket. "You okay to ride?" asked Lucy as Bobby pulled his on. "You two polished off a six-pack and some wine as well."

"We'll drive slow," he promised.

The ride to the Gibbs Hill lighthouse twisted upwards from the South Road. When they finally reached the crest of Gibbs Hill, the view was majestic, even at night. The boys could pick out the twinkling lights of houses and settlements all the way to Hamilton and beyond. Above them, the lighthouse's powerful beacon swept the Bermudian night sky in swooshing arcs. They removed their helmets and sat on a stone wall, enjoying the view.

"I got something for you," said Bobby, producing the cigars and a lighter.

"All right!" cried Barnes. "Couldn't think of a better time to have one." They lit up and blew out billowy clouds. "Great vacation, my man," he said. "It was cool to be free to do what we wanted, away from home. And I think the girls feel the same way. So, tell me: are you getting nervous about the whole getting hitched thing?"

"Kind of," Bobby admitted. "But then I think, Jeez, how can I do any better than Lucy?"

"I agree. She's definitely a keeper. Just as long as you're sure. It's a big step, man."

"I know. But I'm sure." They high-fived, then smoked in silence for a few minutes. Suddenly, Bobby remembered what was in his pocket. "Hey," he said, "I want you to take this."

"What is it?" asked Barnes, lifting an eyebrow. "Your last will and testament?"

"Very funny. Actually, it's, ah, a surprise. Open it when you get home."

"If you say so." They were so mellow at the moment that Barnes probably would've agreed to anything.

"Think we should head back?" said Bobby, noting some clouds that were rolling in from the south.

"I guess so," sighed Barnes. "Hopefully, Tish has sobered up a little. A little late-night farewell-to-Bermuda boom-boom might be in order."

They pulled on their helmets and started up the bikes, as the lights of the island began winking out.

# Chapter Twelve

Bobby had been right the night before; a cold front had swept over Bermuda while they slept. Of course, as this was April, they had been incredibly lucky with the weather so far, experiencing clear, abnormally warm conditions.

At the ungodly hour of 7 AM Barnes rapped on the door, and Bobby and Lucy made themselves presentable to see them off. Since the cycle rental place would be coming by to pick up Barnes's bike later that morning, there wasn't much to do but offer some handshakes and hugs. The envelope wasn't even mentioned, partly because Barnes figured it was between himself and Bobby only.

And also because by that morning, Bobby Romero had forgotten it had even existed.

As their friends' taxi left the parking lot amidst a lot of spirited waving, Bobby asked his fiancée, "Feel like going for breakfast?"

"It's too early," she said. "I think we should go back to bed."

"You don't have to tell me twice," said Bobby.

\* \* \*

The rest of the day was spent alternating between their bedroom and the heated hotel pool, with a cobbled together lunch of cold leftover chicken the only interruption to the young lovers. Somewhere in the midst of this revelry they decided to spend their last night in Hamilton at a pub called the Hog Penny, named after the design on Bermuda's smallest coin. And so, they showered and rode into Hamilton for a final romantic night on the town.

The Hog Penny was as close to an English pub as they were going to get, and its atmosphere was warm and cozy on this cool evening. Bobby ordered a Dark and Stormy, and Lucy a rum Swizzle, to be accompanied by a shepherd's pie and fish and chips, respectively.

Their drinks arrived first and they clinked glasses. "To a great vacation week," he said. They took a sip, and then something seemed to catch Lucy's eye. He turned to see what it was, and spied a fairly young couple at a nearby table with two adorable blonde-haired children, a girl and a boy.

"Cute kids," observed Bobby.

"When I have children, that's what I want," said Lucy. "A couple of towheads."

"What's a towhead?"

"A kid with blonde hair, silly. You've never heard that term?"

"Nope. But, uh, if you haven't noticed, I have fairly dark hair. You still think the kids would come out blonde?"

"Oh yes." She took another sip and smiled. "And while we're talking about such things, what's your take on Barnes and Tish? I mean, you guys have been best friends forever, so how do you see their relationship? Do you think they have a future?"

It was a typical Lucy move. She loved talking about *other* people's relationships. But Bobby had been pondering this question himself after spending a week with the couple. "Well," he said, "as of this moment, Barnes is in love with her. But I've seen him go through phases like this before, all the way back to high school. The thing is, he sees friends of his getting engaged and married—like me, for example—and I guess he's thinking about his own future. But to tell you the truth, I have some serious doubts about them staying together."

"How come?"

"Well, first of all, Barnes is the most generous, most giving guy you'll ever meet, whether it's his buddies or the girls he goes out with. And I think that someday he's going to make a great father. But Tish scares me."

"Why?"

"Because besides obviously being into herself, I don't know if she'd be satisfied with a guy who has a pretty low-level desk job with the phone company. And that's even though she's only a receptionist at a doctor's office herself. I just think the whole family deal with a hard-working husband where she will have to carry part of the load isn't her thing. I wouldn't be surprised if she tries to snag some young doctor, quit working, and join the local country club, where she could spend the day playing tennis and having drinks on the patio."

"Yeah, I kind of feel the same way."

He looked at her. "Lucy, you don't mind that I'm

a football coach, do you? And that I like teaching? I mean, you know I'm never going to be a wealthy guy—"

"Why are you saying this?" she asked with mild annoyance. "You're good at what you do, and you like working with the kids."

"I know," he said, "but I just want to make sure *you're* gonna be happy."

"Don't worry about me," she said reassuringly. "But I would worry about your buddy. From what I can see, he's headed for a disaster."

Later they walked hand-in-hand along Front Street, weaving in and out of throngs of cruise ship tourists, before taking a last drink at Rum Runners and motoring home, finally falling asleep in each other's arms.

* * *

The next morning they awoke, hurriedly packed, settled their tab in the hotel office, and were picked up for their ride to the airport. Neither one said much, lost in their thoughts as the scenery flashed by. Bobby felt that overall, it had been a good vacation. There were a few rough spots, but what young couple didn't have them? He was worried about Barnes, though. Maybe he'd have a talk with him back home at softball practice tomorrow morning.

Their flight was uneventful and smooth, but as they lifted off and the pastel houses of Bermuda faded in the distance, he had an odd feeling that it was the end of something. He attributed it to post-vacation blues.

His brother Joe picked them up at the airport and dropped off Lucy first. They'd all chit-chatted about the trip on the way to her house, but once Bobby had helped her inside and returned to the car, Joe asked, "So how was it *really?* You guys have a good time alone?"

"It was great," he answered. "Can't wait to go back there someday."

# Chapter Thirteen

Bobby's eyes opened shortly before 8 AM the next day, Sunday, which was chilly and damp. The rest of the family, he could tell, was still asleep. His eyes scanned the room he'd called his own for the past fifteen years, since they'd moved to New Rochelle. Pictures from high school and college dotted the walls, mostly football action shots and team photos. Various sports trophies stood proudly on his bookshelves. And on his dresser, front and center, was a photo of himself and Lucy taken the previous year when they had served as chaperones at his school's senior prom. He had worn a three-piece gray suit with a red tie, and her blonde hair shone against an off-the-shoulder, midnight blue dress. He stood behind her, his arms around her waist, and her fingers—not yet displaying the engagement ring—entwined with his. Both were smiling broadly.

He went downstairs to the kitchen and got the coffee maker going, then looked through the refrigerator for breakfast food. Happily, he spied one last square of Entenmann's coffee cake that nobody had gotten to. He poured a steaming cup of coffee into a mug, added a little milk and sugar, and sat down to eat at the kitchen table. Yesterday's *New York Daily*

*News* was on the table, and he immediately turned to the sports section and caught up on the Yankees' early-season woes.

He was just cleaning up after himself when there was a faint tapping on the front door of his parents' split-level home. It was Barnes, and he didn't look happy. "Hey man, you sure are early," Bobby said. "We don't have softball practice till ten. You want some coffee?"

His best friend looked at him strangely, like he was searching his face for some elusive clue to something. "No, that's okay," he said. "Are you alone?"

"Well, yeah," said Bobby. "Everyone's still asleep. You coming in, or what?"

"Yeah, sure," said Barnes. "Let's sit in the kitchen. And on second thought, I'll take that coffee."

"Coming right up." Bobby had brewed an entire pot, and poured Barnes a cup, black with three sugars, the way his friend always took it.

"Thanks," he said as Bobby put it before him. He still had that odd look, though. Then he ran his fingers through his hair. "I don't know where to begin," he said.

Bobby figured Barnes and Tish had had a fight on the way home and said, "Jeez, just spit it out, okay?"

"All right." He took a deep breath. "Bobby, man," he said haltingly, "I'm worried about you."

"*Me?* How come?"

"How *come?* Have you forgotten about the mystery letter you gave me at the lighthouse the other night?"

"Letter? What letter?"

Barnes sighed. "Holy shit, man. You really don't remember?"

Bobby looked at him blankly.

Barnes sighed again. "Okay, man, it's like this: we cooked that big old dinner at the hotel, and then you and I took a motorbike ride to the Gibbs Hill lighthouse to have a cigar—"

"Yeah, I remember that. So what?"

"So what? Christ, you must've been drunk or something, because when we got up there you gave me *this*." He pulled a creased envelope out of his jacket pocket and tossed it on the table in front of Bobby, who stared at it like it was a live grenade.

"Look at it," commanded Barnes gently.

He took the envelope in his hands and read the inscription. The handwriting was his, but it looked pretty shaky:

*Give to Barnes-open back home.*

Bobby looked across the table at Barnes, who quietly said, "Look inside." With trembling fingers he pulled a single sheet of Reefside Apartments stationery from the envelope, and unfolded it. Strange black and yellow starbursts started popping behind his eyes as he tried to focus. He blinked a few times, and then it cleared up. But that didn't make him any less apprehensive to read it:

*Barnes,*

*Please do this for me tomorrow. Go to this address in Yonkers: 55 Overlook Street. See if Valentina Dominguez lives there. It means a lot. Thanks*

Bobby finished reading and slowly lifted his eyes to meet his friend's, which were filled with worry. "Okay," Barnes said calmly. "So, after work I get in my car and drive all the hell the way to Yonkers. I have no freaking clue where Overlook Street is, so I go into a gas station to get directions."

"Did you find it?" asked Bobby, his voice barely a whisper.

"Oh, I found it all right. Not a great part of town, let me tell you. So, I work my way down the street and park in front of 55 Overlook. Except *there is no 55 Overlook*."

"There isn't?"

"No, man. There *was* a pretty large home there, but all I found was a pile of rubble. It seems they'd just finished demolishing it the other day."

"But—"

Barnes held up his hand to stop him. "Let me finish. So then, I actually went next door and rang the doorbell. This old lady answered; she probably thought I was selling something, because she started to close the door on me. So I said, 'Ma'am, I just want to know if Valentina Dominguez used to live in the house next door.' She said, 'Dominguez? Nah, no Dominguez. The O'Malleys lived there for years and years. Then he died, and she went into a nursing home. Now it's tore down. I think they're gonna put a deli there.' Then she shut the door in my face." He rubbed his eyes. "Bobby, what's all this about, man? Some kinda lame April Fool's joke? I don't mind telling you, it was a great big waste of my time. So why did you send me there?"

"I don't know, Barnes," he said helplessly.

"God, I was hoping you wouldn't say that," he replied. "I mean, you weren't totally yourself in Bermuda, I could see that. Even Lucy asked if there was something up with you, but shit, I didn't see something like *this* coming." He dropped his voice so that it was barely audible. "Do you think you should, uh, see someone about all this?"

Bobby's heart was pounding. The embarrassment, coupled with a mystifyingly overwhelming sense of loss, had him near tears; but he sucked it up and fought them back. "Nah, I'm okay, Barnes, really," he said. "I guess it was just something crazy I did when I had too much to drink. I'm sure nothing like it will ever happen again. But, thanks for going there. I really appreciate it."

His friend softened. "Hey, you would've done the same for me," he reasoned. "We're Butch and Sundance, remember?" And he smiled. "Just don't be afraid to ask me for help, or whatever, if you need it in the future."

"Okay. And Barnes?"

"What?"

"I'd appreciate it if, you know, you don't mention this to anyone."

"You got it," he replied. "In fact… " Before Bobby could react, he stood up, strode to the stove, lit the stationery on fire, and then dropped it into the metal sink, where it turned to ash. A jet of water from the faucet, and it was gone. He said, "See you at practice later," clapped Bobby on the shoulder, and saw himself out.

Bobby sat at the table for a long time, trying to get his head around what had just happened. Had the note really been written in a drunken stupor? If so, he had to cut back. But what if it wasn't? And who was Valerie Domingo, or whatever her name was?

# Chapter Fourteen

It was cold at Trinity School field, with the April breeze coming in off Long Island Sound, as the Alums softball team gathered for their first official practice of the '79 season. Some were still in top shape from their football days and, like Bobby, worked out religiously. But a few of the others, primarily the guys who had been linemen in college, had started to let themselves go a bit. Consequently, there was a lot of groaning and complaining as Bobby and Barnes got them into a stretching circle. But it was all good-natured, as the guys had a strong bond forged during their past gridiron wars. Few of them took the softball thing half as seriously as some of the other teams in their league, as it was their physical talent that got them by in most cases. However, barely missing the playoffs the previous season still rankled them.

"How was Bermuda?" asked Nick Nolin, a former defensive tackle who now masqueraded as a first baseman.

"Fannnntastic!" crowed Barnes. "We had a great time. Right, Bobby?"

"Yup," he replied, working his right hamstring. "But it's good to be back. I just wish the weather was better."

"You got that right," echoed Larry Tunney, who had starred at linebacker in college. "You could've at least brought some of that Bermuda sunshine home with you."

When stretching was done they huddled together, some of them sporting hooded sweatshirts and ski caps to go with their softball pants and spikes. "Let's start off light, with some batting practice," suggested Bobby. "Everybody gets ten swings. Go out to your normal positions and then we'll rotate around. Fuzzy, you want to throw BP?"

"Sure," answered Franco Florez, who kicked field goals for the football team but was now their primary softball pitcher.

Everyone jogged out to their positions, and soft-tossed the ball around for a couple minutes while Fuzzy warmed up. Bobby had to grunt a bit as he bent over to field low-skipping grounders on the rock-hard dirt infield, but it felt good to be out there again with the guys. And so began practice, with the whistling wind carrying the pinging sounds of aluminum bats meeting balls, and mindless jock chatter.

As the batting drill progressed, Bobby kept an eye out for Barnes, who was moving among the four outfield positions. His buddy was one of the guys on the team who had played virtually no organized sports outside of football, counting on his athleticism and enthusiasm to get him through on the diamond. But he tended, as was his personality, to overdo it at times, slamming into opposing catchers in plays at the plate and sending infielders cartwheeling when he slid in hard to break up a double play. But it was in the field with his own teammates where Barnes was particularly dangerous. The previous season he'd run full-bore into John Kenny, another outfielder, trying to chase down a ball in the gap between them. Kenny had suffered a dislocated shoulder and was done for the season.

And so, when Nick Nolin, in his turn at bat, swung mightily at an outside pitch and only clipped it, sending a towering pop fly into short right field, Bobby hesitated before going back on the ball. His years of playing the sport had taught him to go after it until he was called off by the outfielder, so he opened his hips and retreated, tracking the ball over his left shoulder and waiting for the right fielder—in this case, Barnes—to call him off. When he didn't hear him, he figured his buddy had been playing too deep and had no chance to make the play, so he kept going, and was just about to yell "I got it!" when Barnes hit him like a runaway train.

* * *

For a few seconds the world swam before Bobby until someone said, "Is he still out?"

"Freakin' Barnes," he murmured, and then realized he was sitting up.Then he heard a female voice say, "You okay, Bobby?" and figured he was being mocked. "Not funny, guys," he managed before opening one eye.

"He's awake!" said Valentina, with a female flight attendant smiling over her shoulder. There was some light applause from behind them. "Oh, honey," she said, kissing him on the forehead, her eyes wet.

"Wh-what happened?" he mumbled. "Where's Barnes?"

"*Barnes?*" she laughed. "Well, he's probably home in New Rochelle right now."

"And Lu-" he stopped short of saying the name.

"Lou? Lou who?" she replied, wiping her eyes.

"Forget it," he said, thinking *Well, THAT was the strangest dream ever*. "Just tell me what happened. Where are we?"

"Okay, so on our way to Bermuda—and directly over the Triangle, I might add—something malfunctioned in the plane, and we were diverting to Charlotte for repairs when we had some bad turbulence and you lost consciousness."

"How long was I out?"

"I don't know, it got pretty wild for a bit. Thirty seconds? Maybe a minute?"

"That's *all?*"

"Uh-huh."

*No, it couldn't have been a dream,* he thought—*I wasn't unconscious long enough for all that to happen.* Then what was it? Had he passed through some kind of portal to a parallel universe, one where he would lose not only Lucy, but Valentina as well, because he messed with fate by trying to confirm his future with her? Whatever it was, the whole 1979 thing had been so real that it shook him. So many things he'd forgotten or deeply buried over the years had come back, and so vividly. And for a moment he was angry at himself for having been such a fool with Lucy. But then again, he had been young and in love... or maybe just in love with the *idea* of being in love, not in love with the girl who would break his heart. One thing was for sure: whatever he'd just experienced, he would never tell a soul, not even Barnes or Val.

They'd think he was nuts, anyway. All that mattered now was that he was fortunate to be back... back where he *belonged.*

He saw that Val was waiting for him to say something, and he managed to ask, "But... uh... everything's okay with the plane?"

"Yeah. It was scary, but the pilot got it under control. So we're going to land in Charlotte and get a new aircraft. I heard one of the crew say we might have to lay over. But then we should be good to go. Here's your hat," she added, picking his Yankees cap off the floor.

"Thanks," he said, putting it on slowly and looking around.

"What's the matter?" she asked. "Are you sure you're alright? Want me to call for—"

"No, no, Val, I'm okay," he said. "Seriously, I'm fine. Just a little shook up. But... would you mind if we didn't go to Bermuda? Maybe somewhere else?"

"How come?"

"I don't know... it just doesn't feel right. At least not right now."

"So you want to go home?"

"No, just somewhere else. *Anywhere* else."

"Okay, then can I pick the destination?"

"Sure. Your choice."

"Hmmm... how about Fiji? We've never been. And it's supposed to be so exotic."

"Fiji it is, then. We'll work it all out when we get to Charlotte. And Val?"

"Yes?"

"Thanks."

"For what?"

"For just… being here."

She playfully raised an eyebrow. "You're funny, Bobby. Where else could I be? But anyway, you're welcome. Oh, look, our drinks are here."

"Sorry about the delay," said the flight attendant. "We were a little out of sorts for a while there. The drinks are on the house, by the way; it's the least we could do for your trouble."

"I don't remember ordering drinks," said Bobby.

"You'd fallen asleep early on, so I ordered for you," said Valentina. She smiled and handed him a Dark and Stormy.

If you enjoyed *A Bermuda Triangle Love Story*, I would like to share with you a preview of my latest full-length novel, *30 Minutes in Memphis: A Beatles Story*. It is available on Amazon in both paperback and Kindle, and endorsed by Beatle fans everywhere, including Mrs. Julia Baird, John Lennon's sister, who graciously collaborated on the title selection.

# Prologue
## August 19, 2016

The woman emerged from her silver Nissan SUV onto the hot macadam surface of a barren parking lot, the car's frigid air-conditioning a stark contrast to the steamy, high 80s climate. She removed the light jacket she'd worn on the long drive to get here and threw it back onto the driver's seat before using the remote to lock up. Then she moved towards the only other car in the lot, a black BMW sedan, some twenty feet away.

A man stood in front of the Beemer, his back to her. She guessed his height at about six-one, with the familiar bony shoulders that caused one to imagine he'd neglected to remove the clothes hanger from his black golf shirt before putting it on. Playfully, she sneaked up on him, but a tap on the shoulder failed to elicit a cry of surprise. Instead, he turned to her and they embraced, the top of her head well below his chin. "I'm glad you came," he murmured into her thick brown hair. The two held each other tightly for a few more seconds, then stood at arm's length, holding hands.

"You look the same," she said, shaking her head in wondrous approval.

"No, I don't," he replied wryly, "but I thank you for making my day."

"I mean it, seriously!" she countered, her accent breaking through to where "I" sounded like "Ah." "Okay, so there's some gray in there, but you've still got that curly mop. But where are your glasses?"

"I switched to contacts long ago, which allow me to see that you, my dear, are as stunning as ever." He perused her with a broad grin. "I'll bet you still play a mean game of tennis. You've cut your hair, though."

"Yeah, that happened around 1990. Figured I was getting too old for the *mod* look. And you don't want to know how gray it'd be without my monthly coloring." She squinted through the hazy sunlight. "Tell you what, though. That ol' thing over there still looks the same." She nodded towards a large object in the distance.

"It's a relic, like us," he joked.

"Speak for y'self."

They shared a laugh and peered across the cracked parking lot at a domed structure resembling a whitewashed spaceship resting on its concrete launchpad—or maybe a half-cooked container of Jiffy Pop.

"I can't believe they haven't torn it down yet," she marveled. "What're they waiting on? It's been vacant for like ten years, I'm told."

"There are all kinds of theories and proposals," he explained. "Some groups want to demolish it for a fairgrounds or recreation complex; some want to restore it. The city government's been wrestling with the problem for years, and they're not getting anywhere. There's another hearing later this month."

She nodded, a trickle of sweat tracking its way down the side of her face. He deftly flicked it aside.

"Thanks," she said, "I almost forgot how god-awful the weather is here in August."

"Betcha it's cooler in there," he said, inclining his head towards the building.

"But it's locked up tight, isn't it?"

He smiled impishly. "Not quite," he gently corrected. "I know a way in."

"Should we?"

"How could we *not*?"

"But won't you, you know, get in some kind of trouble? A guy in your position?"

"Nah," he said with a chuckle. "I've got friends in high places, remember."

"Okay, then," she said conspiratorially. "Let's do it. Lead the way."

Minutes later, after crossing the vast parking lot and skirting the perimeter of the building, the man comically cast furtive glances in both directions, then eased open a service entrance door with a busted lock. "Still want to do it?" he whispered teasingly.

"Why not?" she replied, stepping through the portal into the gloomy darkness of the deserted Mid-South Coliseum. "It's only been fifty years."

# Chapter One
## May, 1966

"Marnie Culpeper, you get your behind down here right now and eat your breakfast before you're late to school!" Tillie's voice bounced off the stairwell walls and reverberated in the bedroom where the fifteen-year-old lay, her long tresses a swirl enveloping her head and blotting out the sun streaming through her window. It never failed; her housekeeper blurted the same warning every single day of the school year. Thank God today was her last one—as a junior high schooler, anyway.

Yawning loudly, Marnie blindly reached out and brought her hand down on a button switch mounted to the top of her nightstand. The button activated a contraption that would have made Rube Goldberg envious; a series of levers and pulleys snaked up the wall behind the nightstand and over to a nearby table where her record player lay, its fliptop open and a shiny vinyl LP awaiting.

A final pulley gently lowered the phonograph needle onto the activated turntable, and the Lennon-McCartney composition "I'll Cry Instead," the first track of the *Something New* album of 1964—the Beatles' fifth release in the States—sprang to life. The record had been selected the night before and carefully slipped from its sheathing that featured a color photograph of the group performing during its historic Ed Sullivan appearance. Marnie had gently set it in place before she took her nightly shower, dried her hair, and brushed it 100 times exactly to bring out the luster, a technique she'd read about in *Seventeen* magazine. Whereas many of her female schoolmates were doing the bouffant thing—along with some holdover beehives, mostly from the "country" crowd—Marnie had gone to the much more "mod" center part favored by British girls, her locks falling halfway down her back. Of course, this often presented a problem, like right now, as it was cocooned around her head.

She sat up and cleared the hair from her face, yawned again, and padded off to the upstairs bathroom where she washed up, sprayed on some deodorant, and brushed her teeth (why, she didn't know; she was going to eat breakfast anyway). Then it was time to slip into her preferred school attire that she sported at Hillcrest Junior High School—namely, a Beatles tee shirt and jeans. Most of the time, though, she did put on a skirt or dress like the other girls, and that was just to get the school administrators, and Tillie, off her back for a while. Besides, she knew the housekeeper was just acting upon orders from The Sarge.

After pulling on her Converse Chuck Taylors, Marnie sat at her overflowing makeup table and ran a brush through her hair. She had an oval face, with a slightly upturned nose and a spray of freckles across her cheeks that made her look younger, though she'd heard the boys at school had classified her as "cute." On this day, besides her sleepy brown eyes staring back at her, the mirror was edged with magazine photos of the four people who were at the epicenter of her life, boys named John, Paul, George and Ringo. In fact, there was scarcely a space on her bedroom walls that *wasn't* occupied by the lads from Liverpool. The only reason they weren't on the ceiling as well was because the scotch tape wouldn't hold in the Memphis humidity.

She spritzed on some Yardley perfume (the brand of choice with British girls), rose from the chair as the last strains of "Any Time at All" drifted across the room, and deftly lifted the needle from the LP before switching off the phonograph (Myles hadn't figured out a way to rig that up yet) and returning the record to its sleeve. Then it was down the stairs in a rush to where Tillie was pouring some Rice Krispies into her official Beatles Fan Club cereal bowl.

"Seriously, Miss Marnie," she chided, "is it so important for you to eat out of a bowl with those bugs on it?" She always called them "those bugs" to get a rise out of her, but it was hard to get mad at Tillie. She was a holdover from Marnie's mom, who had run off with a used car salesman in December of '63, just before the Christmas holiday, no less. Marnie and her dad had been in a bad enough funk over the death of President Kennedy, and although the girl had kind of seen it coming, her mom's desertion had been a jolt nonetheless, a heartless betrayal that had deeply wounded her father and left her embittered.

It was hard to tell how old Tillie was. Her short Afro-bouffant was shot through with gray, but she had a young face of smooth, milk chocolate skin. In her pink housekeeper outfit, she wasn't exactly curvy, more along the lines of "solidly built." Marnie had more than once seen Tillie heft bulging bags of groceries one-handed that she could barely lift with both. And the housekeeper's family situation was kind of mysterious. All Marnie knew about Tillie was that she lived in one of the poorer Negro neighborhoods in town, had a son who was planning to enter the Marine Corps, and twin girls who attended a different school from hers. Tillie's husband was a construction laborer who sometimes went long stretches without work, so this job was important to her, and she was diligent about it if nothing else. And though it was tough for Marnie's dad to retain her services on a policeman's salary, he recognized the woman's value as a stabilizing female influence in his daughter's life. It was Tillie who had guided her through some early boy crushes ("Don't pay him no nevermind, my dear, he ain't deserving of you."), the purchase of her first bra ("Ain't much for it to hold in place now, but if you take after your momma, there will be soon enough."), and her first period ("It's just the Lord's way of reminding you that you're becoming a woman, and that your body is a temple."). Other things, such as shaving her legs and the application of makeup, had been learned through trial and error, with an assist from the columnists of *Seventeen* magazine.

Of course, Tillie's most invaluable role was as a buffer between the flighty teenaged girl and her father. Indeed, there weren't many women who could deal with Sgt. Roy Culpeper without shrinking back or— like Marnie's mom—running off. But Tillie could be just as ornery when she had to, and The Sarge respected that.

"Tillie, you say the same thing every time you make

my cereal," Marnie moaned as she added milk and awaited the famous snap-crackle-pop of the Krispies. "When are you going to accept that the Beatles are here to stay?"

"When the Lord shakes me awake some night and tells me, 'Tillie dear, don't be hard on those bugs, they're just British boys that don't know how silly they look, or how sinful their music is.'"

"Aw, c'mon," Marnie retorted while sipping some fresh squeezed orange juice, "you know as well as I do that their heroes are Negro singers."

"Oh, really? Such as who?"

"Well, Chuck Berry, for one."

"The one been in trouble with the law?"

"And Fats Domino."

"Boy who cain't even control his appetite, and flashes all that gaudy jewelry?"

"How about Little Richard?"

At the mention of this name the housekeeper just rolled her eyes and said, "Don't even get me started on *that* one!"

Marnie couldn't help but laugh. "Okay, okay," she relented, "but they also look up to Elvis. Now c'mon, Tillie, you can't say you don't like Memphis's number one son."

"'Cept he's really from Mississippi. White boy who tries to sing like a colored man, shakin' his hips and whatnot? Hm-mm-mm." She paused for a moment, then softened a bit. "Although he does love his mama, and that's a fact. And when he sets his mind to singing gospel, he's got a right pretty voice. Actually, he's kinda pretty himself, truth be told." She actually arched an eyebrow, which sent Marnie into hysterics.

"But let me point out," Tillie added sternly, catching herself, "he don't look like some girl with a cereal bowl haircut. That boy's served Uncle Sam just like my son's going to, and with a proper haircut, no less!"

Marnie tipped the bowl to her lips and slurped the last of the sweet milk—a habit Tillie detested—and said, "You win, you win. But I still love the lads."

It was while Marnie was at her lowest ebb that she'd first heard "I Want to Hold Your Hand" on WHBQ, the first local radio station to play Elvis's songs a decade earlier. It had been a school morning such as this one, and she was at the breakfast table. For some reason, Tillie had her transistor radio playing on the kitchen counter, when suddenly the woman exclaimed, "What in the *world*?" Strange sounds were emanating from that little box.

Marnie had lifted her head from whatever she was eating. "Turn it up!" she'd said excitedly. What she heard was so new, so fresh and vibrant and *positive*, that she stopped chewing and sat, enraptured, until the conclusion of the song and awaited the motormouthed deejay's comments:

"And those are the Beatles, spelled with an A, the new pop combo who are stirring things up in the British Isles and finding their way onto the charts here in the US of A. We've been getting numerous requests to play their songs, and there's no better place to hear your fabulous faves than Boss Radio WHBQ, so here's another one from the lads from Liverpool called 'All My Loving'!"

She was inextricably hooked. And while it was true that Marnie Culpepper had religiously read *Tiger Beat* and other teen magazines for info on such early 60s teen idols as Fabian and Frankie Avalon and had enjoyed the tunes of vocal groups like the Four Seasons, Beach Boys, and even some Motown acts like the Supremes and Temptations, this was something utterly different. Something that reached into her chest and flooded her heart. *Something to hold onto.*

These guys were cute, with their matching haircuts, Edwardian suits and Beatle boots. But they were also witty and personable, not to mention that they could sing up a storm—in short, everything the twelve-year-old Marnie would want in a boy. So, when it was announced that the Beatles would be coming to the US for a tour commencing with an appearance on the *Ed Sullivan Show* on February 9, 1964, Marnie and her dad tuned in on their Magnavox black and white TV, as did much of America, to see what all the fuss was about.

Predictably, their reactions ran along generational lines. Roy Culpeper, Korean War combat veteran and sergeant in the Memphis PD, a crewcut, spit-and-polish, no nonsense guy whose taste ran to Hank Williams and Buck Owens, was understandably appalled. "I'm missing *Bonanza* for *this*?" he'd moaned. "Are those guys or gals?"

"Oh, Daddy, stop," she'd replied in her most disarming little-girl voice. "They have suits and ties on. I think they're cute."

"Kittens are cute. Boys are supposed to be handsome... and manly."

"I think *you're* cute, Daddy," she'd offered, which made him smile and shake his cinderblock-shaped head.

"Well, at least they can carry a tune," he'd conceded grudgingly. "Ah, well, no harm done, darlin'. They're just a passing fad, you'll see."

But he was wrong, at least where his daughter was concerned. Because while the Beatles quickly became popular at Marnie's school (prompting quickly instituted rules outlawing hairstyles on boys that covered their ears or fell below the tops of their shirt collars) Marnie took it to another level, becoming totally immersed in everything Beatle. She saved enough from her meager allowance to buy every teen magazine or piece of paraphernalia that had a Beatles likeness on it. Record albums and 45s were requested as special birthday or Christmas gifts. And her viewings of *A Hard Day's Night* and *Help!* at the local movie house were so numerous for Marnie (most of the time accompanied by her best friend, Charlotte Perkins, whose passion for the boys was not nearly as fervent) that she had pretty much memorized the dialogue from both films and quoted from them frequently, her Southern drawl mixing awkwardly with the Fabs' Liverpudlian lilt.

Of course, when her obsession with the group did not wane, everyone who was associated with Marnie, including her father, teachers and classmates, began to wonder if this was all a giant compensation for the loss of her mother, an escape from reality of sorts. The only person who seemed to "get it" was her friend Myles Goldfarb, architect of her record player apparatus. Like her, Myles, one of the first boys to be reprimanded when his curly dark hair began to hang too low for the junior high administration's taste, was considered a bit odd, both because he was virtually the only Jew in their class—a New York transplant, no less—and because he seemingly went out of his way to tweak the "squares" who made up the majority of the student population. When he wasn't getting beaten up, that is.

The doorbell rang, and Tillie glanced at the clock over the sink. "That would be your partner in crime," she said. "Time to get cracking."

With a quick goodbye Marnie scooped up her books and bolted out the front door into the muggy humidity where her best friend awaited.

"'Bout time, sleepyhead," teased Charlotte, attired in her customary conservative skirt and blouse. Her parents were quite active in the Baptist church Marnie and her father attended. Charlotte's dad also owned the local supermarket where the girls were to be employed this upcoming summer as cash register baggers. Like Marnie, she was slight of build (but blonde) and quite athletic, and the two frequently studied together to maintain their A- averages. They trusted each other with their secrets, and boys were a frequent topic.

However, though she was understanding of Marnie's preoccupation with the Beatles, the opinions of other less tolerant classmates bothered Charlotte, and more than once this past year she'd had to ask her best friend to tone it down a bit when she'd start expounding on the virtues of the Fab Four's music. "Y'all aren't ever gonna have boys ask you out if you spend all your time mooning over the Beatles," she'd recently counseled.

"I know, you're right," Marnie had answered. "I get carried away sometimes."

Today their conversation on the twenty-minute walk to school centered on report cards and summer plans. Both expected to do well academically and looked forward to the cookouts and outings at the lake that would commence with Memorial Day this coming weekend.

"You think Tommy Plummer will ask you out this weekend at the church picnic?" Marnie asked. "He's been making eyes at you this past month in English class."

"I think that's a good possibility," Charlotte said confidently. "I wouldn't mind going out with the future quarterback of the varsity, would you?"

"Guess not. It's just that he's, well, y'know, kinda—"

"Square? Clean cut? Is that it? Well, I'll be honest with you, I don't mind at all. He comes from a good family, who has lots of money, by the way. If he wants to spend some of it on this little girl, I'm not gonna stop him."

The two laughed.

"And what about Myles, Marnie? Do you like him?"

"We're just friends," she stated primly. "He's a good guy. The fact that he's Jewish doesn't mean much to me, though my dad probably wouldn't approve. Anyway, a girl can have guy friends, you know, without it being romantic."

"Still holding out for Paul?" Charlotte teased. "John's married, you know, with a son—"

"Will you *stop*, please? I just haven't met the right guy yet, Char. Maybe this summer."

"Yeah, Marnie, the possibilities will be *endless* at the checkout counter. Maybe Prince Charming will stop in for a can of tuna fish."

\* \* \*

Even though the last day of school was only a half session, it was still a drag. Time to clean out lockers and say goodbye to one's friends and teachers for the summer. Of course, to keep a lid on the place the students' report cards were to be distributed in homeroom at the very end of the day. As expected, Marnie had gotten a B in math, her hardest subject, and As the rest of the way, which was one reason her dad went easy on her with the Beatles stuff. Still, The Sarge had no aspirations of a college career for his daughter. A secretarial job with some company—while she looked for a husband, of course—was more the norm in his world. It didn't matter that Marnie's mom had been a secretary as well, for the man she'd eventually run off with.

Marnie was tossing out the last of the old bagged lunches that had been decomposing in the bottom of her locker when she felt a familiar tap on the shoulder. Marnie had long since ceased to be spooked when Myles sneaked up on her. In fact, it was their usual way of saying hello.

"Wow, how old is *that* one?" he said, wrinkling his nose. "My guess is baloney and mayo."

"Close. It's ham," she replied, peeking inside for a second. "Or it *was*." Marnie noticed her friend looked a little out of sorts. "S'matter, Myles," she said, "you pull an F in science or something?"

"Uh, no," he answered, taking off his tortoise shell glasses for a quick polish.

"Somebody pickin' on you again?"

"Uh-uh, not today."

"Well, that's an improvement. So, what's up?"

He pulled an envelope from his back pocket and held it out, his face flushing red. "Uh, happy birthday," he said.

"It's not for another week, Myles."

"Yeah, I know, but I might not see you next week. Would you just open it?"

She frowned good-naturedly while tearing off the end. "Jeez Louise, Myles, you didn't have to get me a—"

"Careful!" he hissed.

She gave him a suspicious look, then slowly peeled off the rest of the envelope's corner and reached inside. There was, indeed, a card from the five and dime, simply signed *Hope you like it, Myles*. But it was what was *inside* the card that took her breath away: an orange cardboard ticket with red and black lettering for a Beatles concert to be held on Friday, August 19, at the Memphis Mid-South Coliseum at 8:30 PM. The price on the ticket was $5.50. Marnie, usually at no loss for words, was dumbstruck. "What... how... " was all she could manage.

Myles held up a hand to stop her. "It was just announced," he explained. "They're doing a foreign tour first, and then coming to the US. Well, as you know, my dad's pretty well-connected, so it was fairly easy for him—"

He never got to finish his explanation (which included the fact that he was the owner of a second ticket) because Marnie grabbed him around the waist and started twirling him in the semi-crowded hallway until they finally collapsed in a laughing heap on the beige linoleum floor.

If the Beatles had a birthday song, she would have sung it out loud.

# About the Author

Paul Ferrante is originally from the Bronx and grew up in the town of Pelham, New York. He received his undergraduate and Master's degrees in English from Iona College, where he was also a halfback on the Gaels' undefeated 1977 football team. Paul has been an award-winning secondary school English teacher and coach for over 35 years, as well as a columnist for *Sports Collector's Digest* magazine since 1993 on the subject of baseball ballpark history. Many of his works can be found in the archives of the National Baseball Hall Of Fame in Cooperstown, NY. His writings have led to numerous radio and television appearances related to baseball history.

Paul's young adult **T.J. Jackson Mysteries** series has led him to speak at the 150th Anniversary Battle Commemoration in Gettysburg, PA, and the National Baseball Hall Of Fame during their 75th Anniversary celebration.

Paul lives in Stratford, Connecticut and Vero Beach, Florida with his wife Maria and daughter Caroline, a film screenwriter/director.

Please visit Paul's website for information on the **T.J. Jackson Mysteries** and his other writings. Also stop by T.J. Jackson's Facebook page.

www.paulferranteauthor.com
https://www.facebook.com/tjjacksonmysteries/

# Also by Paul Ferrante

## With Fire & Ice Young Adult Books

<u>The T.J Jackson Mysteries</u>
*Last Ghost at Gettysburg*
*Spirits of the Pirate House*
*Roberto's Return*
*Curse of the Fairfield Witch*
*The Voodoo Cult's Treasure*

## Adult Novels with Melange Books
*The Rovers: a Tale of Fenway*